The Holy Innocents

MIGUEL DELIBES

The Holy Innocents

A NOVEL

Translated from the Spanish by Peter Bush

Foreword by Colm Tóibín

A MARGELLOS
WORLD REPUBLIC OF LETTERS BOOK

Yale UNIVERSITY PRESS | NEW HAVEN & LONDON

The Margellos World Republic of Letters is dedicated to making
literary works from around the globe available in English through
translation. It brings to the English-speaking world the work of
leading poets, novelists, essayists, philosophers, and playwrights
from Europe, Latin America, Africa, Asia, and the Middle East to
stimulate international discourse and creative exchange.

Yale University Press books may be purchased in quantity for
educational, business, or promotional use. For information, please
e-mail sales.press@yale.edu (U.S. office) or sales@yaleup.co.uk
(U.K. office).

Set in Source Serif type by Motto Publishing Services.
Printed in the United States of America.

Library of Congress Control Number: 2024944708
ISBN 978-0-300-27513-1 (paperback : alk. paper)

A catalogue record for this book is available from the
British Library.

This paper meets the requirements of ANSI/NISO Z39.48-1992
(Permanence of Paper).

10 9 8 7 6 5 4 3 2 1

In memory of my friend
Félix Rodríguez de la Fuente

Contents

Foreword

In his book *My Last Sigh,* the film director Luis Buñuel, who was born in Aragón in 1900, wrote about the rural Spain of his youth: "The respectful subordination of the peasants to the big landowners was deeply rooted in tradition and seemed unshakeable . . . Agriculture was semi-feudal; tenant farmers worked the land and gave half their harvest to their proprietors."

Buñuel's biographer John Baxter noted: "The señoritos and señoritas of the landed gentry were left to live as they saw fit . . . Some señoritos were pious, others drunks and rapists."

In 1933, Buñuel made his documentary film *Las Hurdes,* also known as *Land Without Bread,* about peasant life in a remote part of the province of Extremadura: "I didn't find a single drawing, nor a song, nor a firearm," he wrote. "At the same time they don't make bread. It was an almost neolithic culture, without folklore, nor artistic manifestation of any sort. The sole tool which they possessed was the plough." The peasants suffered from malnutrition. On the first day of filming, Buñuel addressed the crew: "Do you see this wonderful valley? Well, this is where hell begins."

Buñuel went into exile after the Civil War, which lasted

from 1936 to 1939; many Spanish artists scattered then. In 1939, for example, the composer Manuel de Falla fled to Argentina, where he died in 1946. The cellist Pau (Pablo) Casals moved to the United States. The poets Miguel Hernández and Antonio Machado died soon after the war ended. Others experienced a worse fate. The poet Federico García Lorca was murdered by the Nationalist forces in 1937.

Between 1939, when Franco's rule began, and 1975, when the dictator died, cultural life in Spain might thus have been a kind of desert. It is strange, then, to read an account of literary Spain between 1936 and 1950 by the novelist Miguel Delibes (1920–2010) in which he describes a group of novelists who, like himself, published in Spain and remained in the country during the years of the dictatorship. These, loosely part of a group known as the Generation of 1936, included Camilo José Cela (1916–2002), José María Gironella (1917–2003), Carmen Laforet (1921–2004), Ángel María de Lera (1912–1984), and Ana María Matute (1925–2014).

Staying did not mean that these writers collaborated with the regime or became official artists, even though some of them, including Delibes himself and Cela and Gironella, as very young men, had been on the Nationalist side in the Civil War. Once the war was over, however, repression was matched with disillusion, and this was felt deeply by novelists who sought to explore life in a country where fear was matched by complacency, where poverty and underdevelopment were rampant.

While novelists in Spain in these years were, to some extent, exiles in their own country, and some of their books were heavily censored, they were not treated as enemies of the state. Cela and Delibes and Matute, for example, became members of the Royal Spanish Academy during the Franco regime.

For a novelist in Franco's Spain, a private, bookish life was possible. Although there was no question of publishing anything openly critical of the regime, there was more than a semblance of normality in the literary world. Literary magazines and literary prizes existed, for example, including the Premio Nadal, inaugurated in 1944 and funded by the publishing house Destino. It was awarded on January 6 each year for the best unpublished novel. Laforet won the 1944 prize for her novel *Nada,* Gironella won in 1946, Delibes won in 1947 for his first novel, and Matute won the prize in 1959.

The mixture of freedom and repression created a Spanish novel of the dictatorship that was formally adventurous or offered unusual settings or imposed unusual restrictions on itself, using the fabulous or the outlandish rather than mere realism or definite, sharply described social settings.

While these Spanish novelists of the mid-century could often pose as conservative, their style as novelists could be playful, experimental, and strange. Since life for them was never simple, the fiction they wrote was not simple either. Cela, who won the Nobel Prize in Literature in 1989, worked as a state censor at the beginning of the Franco regime and later operated as a police informer. He seemed to be integrated into the machinery of Franco's Spain. Nonetheless, his novel *The Hive* (1951) had to be published in Buenos Aires since it was banned in Spain.

Something unsettling and paradoxical affected the very tone of Cela's book—confident, loud, darting, lacking piety, paying no homage to any set of fixed or established procedures for how a novel might be constructed.

In 1970, Miguel Delibes began to publish a weekly column in the Spanish magazine *Destino*. Over the previous two decades, he had published a book almost every year, including novels, literary criticism, and works on fishing and hunting. As a journalist and editor in the 1950s, he had fought many battles against the censor. Now, at the age of fifty, he seemed relaxed, amused by the world, almost content, even if he was posing as world-weary and reclusive.

In his 1970 diary, he reported that he had turned down an offer from the University of Southern California of twenty thousand dollars for an eight-month teaching stint. He had, he wrote, enough to live on, and even though the money sounded good, accepting would have been to "embrace that consumer society" that he often criticized.

Though encouraged to speak more in public, especially to visiting foreigners, he felt he had less and less to say. That did not prevent him from making clear in one of his columns that he supported the trade union movement. But what animated him the most were days spent trout fishing and evenings spent reading novels by such contemporaries as Gabriel García Marquez, Mario Vargas Llosa, and Saul Bellow, all of whom he admired.

Delibes put much thought into the novel form itself. In August 1970, for example, addressing a conference of foreign students in Burgos, he suggested that his own method had been to refine various systems of narrative rather than reject them. In his novels, he said, he did not set out in advance to create a work that was avant-garde but allowed the theme itself to suggest the form.

In October 1970, when José Varela Ortega, the grandson of the philosopher Ortega y Gasset, came to visit, he and

Delibes discussed the world of the Castilian peasant. "Hurry up and write your novels," the visitor said. "Rural Castile is disappearing."

Since the members of the Generation of 1936 who were novelists did not have a stable world to reflect or explore or re-create, they had to adapt narrative forms and systems to their own particular conditions. They would play, for example, with chronology. They would constrict the time spans they worked with, and indeed the very spaces their characters inhabited. They would avoid, in the main, what was elaborate and panoramic and deal with what was intimate and strange. Or they would offer a version of society that was close to a parody or a dream or a crazy fable.

Cela's *The Hive* took place over a mere few days in 1943. Rather than dramatizing a family or a society, it dealt with the activities of three hundred different characters. It proceeded with self-aware energy. Rather than offering a portrait of a society, the novel demands that narrative tone itself, in all its variety and pliability, appear on display as a kind of protagonist.

So, too, the masterpiece that Miguel Delibes produced in 1966, *Five Hours with Mario,* in which a woman addressed her dead husband as he lay in his coffin. It was set in a circumscribed space, in a confined time. Although many characters were invoked, the novel depended on a solo voice, a single, intense perspective. The monologue form allowed anything at all to be expressed, including the most rambling thoughts and the most structured grievances. Carmen, in the novel, was speaking her mind, but no one was destined to listen, since her husband, the only other presence, was dead. Her words, so elaborate and passionate, fell on deaf ears.

With each book Miguel Delibes wrote, he seemed to be seeking a new form, some of them slyly minimalist. In 1969, he published his novel *The Hedge,* in which the protagonist was employed copying out long lists of zeroes. The strangeness of the novel became even more pronounced when punctuation marks, such as periods and commas and parentheses, were replaced by the actual words for these marks—"period," "comma," "parenthesis"—which were placed in the text beside other words, more normal ones. (In his diary for 1970, Delibes discovered that the American poet e. e. cummings had used the same system, a system Delibes thought he had invented. It proved, he wrote, that "there is nothing new under the sun.")

Five years later, in his novel *The War of Our Ancestors,* Delibes used the form of a simple stark dialogue between two men—a psychiatrist and a peasant found guilty of murder. And he increased the time span from five hours, as in *Five Hours with Mario,* to seven days. The two men could, in the stark narrative system chosen, explore many difficult and random subjects. The dialogue in the novel is presented like a theater script, but with no stage directions. It is like a set of transcribed interviews. The characters do not have thoughts; instead, they make statements and offer responses and ask questions. Like the *Mario* book, the novel depends on voice.

In 1981, Delibes—now in his early sixties—was living and writing in a newly democratic Spain. He might now have felt free to dramatize the subjects that had long been forbidden, most notably the brutality of the Civil War itself, which had shocked him at the time, or indeed the clashes of ideology in the dark period afterward in Spain. (He would write about the Civil War in a later novel—*Stuff of Heroes*—in 1987.)

Instead, he wrote *The Holy Innocents,* a short novel that was close to a fable, using brief scenes, much clipped dialogue, and a plain style. Its power arose by implication, by the use of humor, gentle irony, and immense restraint.

The novel takes us back to the very same harsh and unforgiving landscape as in Buñuel's *Las Hurdes,* virtually unchanged despite the decades between *Las Hurdes* and *The Holy Innocents.* It is as though we have ventured into some place that has been protected from social and political change—indeed, from any form of modernity. The landlord is king. Those beneath him are open to his whims; they are treated as serfs or as animals. But other whims are at play, especially those of Azarías, an oddly deranged figure who can tame birds. His very lack of good sense gives him a kind of power that no one else in the novel has. He also has some comic moments, such as when he begins to count and, on reaching eleven, moves instantly to "forty-three, forty-four, forty-five."

There are moments when the novel could be set in medieval Europe. But then we notice a tractor, "a brand-new red imported tractor." There is also a Mercedes car. And Franco, who is mentioned as a potentate. When Azarías is asked what happened to another character, he replies: "He died, Franco sent him to heaven." And when he is asked when that was, he replies: "A long time ago, when the Moors were here." Elsewhere a character says a partridge flew "faster than any airplane."

In an argument about culture, one guest says that central Europe was more cultured. Señorito Iván, the landlord, replies, "There are no illiterates here now, or do you think we're still in '36?"

What ensues is one of the most telling scenes in all of

Delibes's work. Señorito Iván, in front of his guests, asks the tenants who are present to demonstrate that they can write their names. Régula, the wife of Shorty Paco, "had trouble gripping the pen with her flat, stubby thumb with no fingerprint, yet haltingly, she still managed to write her name." Her thumb, it seems, is "as flat as a spatula." When a guest stares at the thumb, astonished, Señorito Iván "noticing how shocked he seemed, explained, 'Ah you know, the thumbs of the women working with esparto grass are like that . . . it comes with the job, their fingers are deformed by all the grass braiding, it can't be helped . . .'"

Delibes was interested in shooting birds. In the 170 pages of his published diaries from 1970, the word *perdiz* (partridge) and the word *codorniz* (quail) are each mentioned seventeen times.

Shorty Paco in *The Holy Innocents,* unlike Señorito Iván, has a relationship with the land and an uncanny knowledge of where birds can be sought when they have been shot and injured or killed. His knowledge makes him essential to his landlord, who takes the view that among his guests, "everyone who grabbed a hunting gun was a fag except for him."

The hunting outings become a ritual and soon a theater of cruelty as Señorito Iván exerts his power and displays his powerlessness. Loyalty to him by one generation is steadily replaced by a kind of surliness. This culminates, it seems, when Shorty Paco's son refuses the tip of a hundred-peseta note, and when it is pressed on him by the landlord, he responds, "I already said thanks but no thanks." When this exchange is recounted over dinner, the Minister to whom he is complaining announces that "a crisis of authority is affecting every level of society today."

Delibes's genius is to allow us to feel that the proper ending for this novel will be some kind of revolt or set of retaliations, that the peasants will take over the landlord's house and lay waste to his properties. From a passing mention of the Second Vatican Council, we can assume that the story is set in the 1960s, when the entire oppressed population could even, in an act of pure defiance, move to a nearby city.

But Delibes allows nothing so simple to occur. Like the peasants in the novel, he has not been waiting all this time to do something obvious and predictable. In scenes where he could easily paint in bright colors, he is almost reticent, tactful. He wishes the narrative to conceal as much as it reveals. Gradually we sense that a pure order is perhaps not to be disturbed. Perhaps, after all, *The Holy Innocents* is not to be a story about change. And then, stealthily, the two parts of the narrative join in an unexpected culmination. A lord of misrule emerges to disturb the peace and kill the giant. He was there all along. In a most perfect ending, we watch chaos merging with the end of an old regime. It is a kind of justice, as much as the fable will allow.

Colm Tóibín

Book One
Azarías

Azarías's attitude upset his sister Régula and she'd scold him, after which he'd return to La Jara, to the señorito's;* Azarías's attitude upset his sister Régula because she wanted her children to get an education, which her brother thought was a mistake, because,

they'll be no use, they'll end up neither fish nor fowl,

he pontificated in his slightly nasal, garbled speech, and, in any case, at the señorito's in La Jara, nobody cared whether any of them could read or write, whether they were literate or illiterate, nor did they care if Azarías wandered around barefoot mumbling to himself, with patches on his knees and on the seat of his corduroy pants and his fly unbuttoned, and if he suddenly went off to his sister's and the señorito asked after him, and the señorito was told,

he's at his sister's, señorito,

the señorito didn't blink, didn't get angry, maybe he stiffened his left shoulder for a second, but he didn't ask again or react to the news, and when Azarías returned, it was no different,

Azarías is back, señorito,

*Translator's note: A "señorito" is the son of a wealthy landowner who doesn't have to work and can spend his time hunting, drinking, and living in leisure while ordering his social inferiors about.

and the señorito managed a half-hearted smile, for the only thing that really annoyed him was when Azarías claimed he was just one year older than the señorito, because the truth was, Azarías was already a big strong boy when the señorito was born, but Azarías didn't remember that, and if every once in a while Azarías said he was only a year older than the señorito, it was because Dacio the Pigman had said so on New Year's Eve when he was tipsy, and the idea had embedded itself in Azarías's head, so whenever they asked,

how old are you, Azarías?
he'd reply,

a year to the day older than the señorito,
not out of any ill will, or a fondness for lying, but merely because he was simple, and the señorito was wrong to fly off the handle and call him a two-faced liar, especially since instead of walking around the farmstead every blessed day mumbling to himself and chewing his tongue or staring at the nails on his right hand, Azarías now polished the señorito's car with a yellow cloth, and even unscrewed the tops from the tire valves of the señorito's friends' cars so the señorito would always have a good supply if one day things went downhill and there was a shortage, and if that wasn't enough, Azarías took care of his dogs—the retriever and the setter and the three foxhounds—and if, in the depths of night, the shepherd's mastiff howled in the copse of holm oaks or the dogs made a racket, he, Azarías, would soothe them with gentle words and scratch them hard between the eyes until they calmed down and went to sleep, and at first light he'd stretch and yawn and head to the yard, he'd open the front gate to let the turkeys into their enclosure behind the metal fence among the holm oaks, and then he'd sweep out their coops and wa-

ter the geraniums and the weeping willow, and after that he'd clean out the eagle owl's little den and stroke it between the ears, and when night fell, everyone knew that Azarías would sit on the wooden bench by the fire in the bare hallway and pluck the partridges or woodcocks or turtledoves or grouse that the señorito had hunted during the day, and sometimes, if there were a lot, Azarías would give one to his eagle owl, and when the bird saw him coming, its round yellow gaze enveloped him, and it clicked its beak (it hissed at everyone else, the señorito included, and bared its claws like a cat), but it treated Azarías differently, and most nights when there wasn't a tastier tidbit, Azarías would give it a magpie, or a buzzard, or half a dozen sparrows he'd caught with mistletoe bait in the pond (the one with the carp, or God knows where), but in any case, Azarías soothed his Grand Duke whenever it sidled up to him, saying, his voice soft and velvety,

pretty kitey, pretty kitey,

and he scratched its eyebrows and smiled at it with his toothless gums, and if it was time to tie it to the top of the rocky outcropping so the señorito or the señorita (or his friends or her friends) concealed in the blind could have a party and shoot buzzards or crows, Azarías would roll a piece of red flannel around its right leg so the chain didn't rub it sore, and while the señorito or the señorita (or his female friends or her male friends) stayed in the blind, Azarías would wait, crouching in the undergrowth beneath the lookout, swaying like a blade of grass and keeping watch over the Grand Duke, and though he was a little hard of hearing, as he heard each and every gun blast, he shuddered and shut his eyes, and when he opened them again, he looked up at the eagle owl, and when he saw that it was unharmed, standing there erect and defiant, silhouetted above the rocky crag, he was so very proud, and mumbled to himself,

pretty kitey,

and longed to scratch it behind the ears, and the moment the señorito or the señorita or his friends or her friends tired of killing buzzards and crows and came out from the blind, stretching and limbering up as if emerging from a mine shaft, he walked over to the Grand Duke, working his jaw up and down as if chewing something, and the eagle owl preened, so pleased with itself, and stuck out its chest like a peacock, and Azarías smiled,

you weren't even scared, kitey,

he told it, and scratched its head, and finally picked up the dead buzzards, one after another, tied them to the pole, carefully unchained the eagle owl and placed it in the big wooden cage that he lifted onto his shoulders, and, easy does it, walked back to the farm without waiting for the señorito or the señorita (or his men friends or her women friends), who walked slowly and lazily behind him on the path, chatting and gossiping and laughing inanely, and the second he entered the house, Azarías hung the pole from the thick beam in the hallway and released the eagle owl into its den, and when night began to fall, he squatted on the pebbles in the yard, in the white light from the oil lamp, plucked a buzzard, carried it to the window of the eagle owl's den, and went,

woo-oo-oo,

deepening his voice as low as he could, and immediately the eagle owl flew serenely to the bars, in a flurry of wings as gentle and soft as wool, and responded,

woo-oo-oo,

repeating Azarías's woo-oo-oo like an echo from beyond the grave, then it grasped the buzzard between its huge claws and gobbled it down quickly and quietly, and as Azarías watched it eating, he whispered, with a drop of drool escaping his smile,

pretty kitey, pretty kitey,

and once the Grand Duke had finished its feast, Azarías walked to where the señorito's lady friends and the señorita's male friends had parked their cars, he patiently unscrewed the tops from their tire valves, clumsily turning his fingers, and, when he'd finished, he put them alongside the ones he kept in the shoebox in the stables, sat down, and started counting them,

one, two, three, four, five . . .

and after eleven, he'd invariably go,

forty-three, forty-four, forty-five . . .

then he walked out into the pitch-black yard and peed on his hands in the corner so they didn't chap, he fanned the air for a while to get rid of the smell, and life went on like this day after day, month after month, year after year, for a whole lifetime, but despite his methodical routines, at daybreak Azarías would sometimes wake up feeling weak and limp, and on such days he didn't sweep out the chicken coops or put out food for the dogs or clean the eagle owl's den, no sir, he went out into the flax fields or the pig sties or, if the sun was blistering down, into the shade of the arbutus, and when Dacio asked,

what's up, Azarías?

he'd say,

I've got the lazy bug,

and he'd let the dead time pass, and if the señorito came across him and asked,

what's gotten into you, for Chrissake?

Azarías repeated,

I've got the lazy bug, señorito,

and without budging, stretched out among the flax or in the shade of the arbutus, motionless and curled inward, his thighs touching his belly, his elbows pulled in to his chest, he lay there trying not to dribble, or moaning softly like a puppy in need of milk, staring at the blue-green mountains silhouetted against the sky and the round shepherds' huts and behind them the Cerro de las Corzas (and Portugal just beyond), the crags crouching like giant turtles, and the raucous, elongated flight of the cranes heading toward the reservoir, the merino sheep frolicking with their lambs, and if ever Dámaso the Shepherd stopped by and asked,

something wrong, Azarías?

he'd reply,

I've got the lazy bug,

and there he would lie until he felt a sudden urge to drop a load by the arbutus or in a dark crack in the stony ground, and after he relieved himself, his energy would slowly return, and once he'd recovered, he would visit the eagle owl and speak softly between the bars in the window,

pretty kitey,

and the eagle owl kept preening and clicking its curved beak until Azarías gave it a plucked buzzard or woodcock, and so as not to waste time while it devoured the bird, Azarías went over to the stables, sat on the ground, and started counting the valve tops in the box,

one, two, three, four, five . . .

till he reached eleven, then went,

forty-three, forty-four, and forty-five,
and when he finished, he put the lid back on the box, sat and
inspected the stubby nails on his right hand, chomped his
gums, and mumbled to himself, and suddenly decided,

I'm going to my sister's,
and on the porch, he passed the señorito, dozing on the
lounge chair,

I'm going to my sister's, señorito,
and the señorito's left shoulder stiffened ever so slightly before he said,

God be with you, Azarías,
and Azarías went off to the neighboring farm, to his sister's,
and the second she opened the front gate, Régula said,

what did you forget now?
and Azarías,

how are the boys?
and she,

they're at school, where'd you think they'd be?
and Azarías stuck out the tip of his fat pink tongue for a second, then licked the roof of his mouth and said,

you'll be the worse for it, they'll end up neither fish
nor fowl,
and Régula,

did I ask you for your opinion?
but as soon as the sun set, Azarías dozed off by the dying fire,
chewing his tongue, and after some time, he straightened
his head and suddenly said,

tomorrow I'll go back to the señorito's,
and just before dawn broke, the moment the orange stripes
in the firmament lit up the contours of the mountains,

Azarías was already on the road, and four hours later, sweaty and starving, as soon as he heard Lupe sliding the big bolt on the front gate, he was already chanting,

pretty kitey, pretty kitey,

over and over, never letting up, with not so much as a hello to Lupe, who took care of the pigs, and if the señorito was still in bed, the moment the señorito appeared in the hallway, Lupe gave him the news,

Azarías came in the early hours, señorito,

and the señorito screwed up his bleary eyes,

oh, he did, did he?

he said, and his left shoulder stiffened in resignation or surprise, although Azarías could already be heard mucking out the chicken coops or cleaning out the Grand Duke's den and dragging the wooden pail over the pebbles in the yard, and weeks went by like this until one fine day, just before spring, a change came over Azarías, a slow smile spread across his face, and when the sun set, instead of counting valve tops, he grabbed the eagle owl and brought it to the copse of holm oaks, and with the huge, motionless bird perched on his forearm, he peered all around, and as darkness fell, it flew off silently and soon returned with a rat or a finch between its claws, and right there, next to Azarías, it devoured its prey while he scratched its head and listened to the heartbeat of the mountain range, the sad hoarse bark of a fox in heat, or the roars of the rutting stags on the Coto de Santa Ángela, and now and then he'd ask,

the fox is on the prowl, kitey, can you hear her?

and the eagle owl's round yellow pupils glowed in the shadows, and it slowly pricked up its ears and started eating again, and, though not on that occasion, in the springtime they sometimes heard wolves howling, but ever since the electricity men had come and installed posts and wires all across the hillside, they hadn't heard them, and in their place the screeches of a tawny owl punctuated the long silences, and in these moments the Grand Duke raised its enormous head and pricked up its ears, and Azarías laughed noiselessly, whispering,

are you scared, kitey? tomorrow I'm going on a tawny owl chase,

and just as he said, the next day at twilight he headed toward the mountain all alone, cutting a path between blooming rockroses and boxthorn and rocky outcroppings, because the tawny owl cast a kind of spell on Azarías, a strange dark fascination, a kind of frantic infatuation, so when he paused in the middle of the bracken, he could hear his heart pounding, and he waited to catch his breath and calm his racing mind before finally shouting,

hey! hey!

calling to it, calling the tawny owl, and he listened keenly for a reply while the moon peered out from behind the clouds and flooded the landscape with a shadowy phosphorescent haze, and, feeling daunted, he cupped his hands and repeated defiantly,

hey! hey!

until suddenly, twenty yards below, from a stout holm oak, came the longed-for blood-curdling cry,

hoo! hoo!

and when he heard it, Azarías lost himself, lost all notion of time, and burst into a crazy run, grunting, trampling the broom, scratching his face on the lowest branches of the arbutus and cork oaks, and behind him the implacable tawny owl hopped lithely from tree to tree, howling and cackling, and whenever it cackled, Azarías's pupils dilated, his hair stood on end, and he remembered his kitey in the stables and ran even faster, and behind him the tawny owl screeched and cackled again, and Azarías ran and ran; stumbling, picking himself up, he fell and he got up, never looking back, and when he reached the fields, panting breathlessly, Lupe crossed herself,

and where might you be coming from?
and Azarías with a tiny smile, like a kid caught misbehaving, said,

from chasing the tawny owl,
and she retorted,

Jesus Christ! your face looks like Our Lord's on the cross, but he was already in the stables, wiping the blood from his scratches, gasping and drooling, his heart pounding, and after a while, feeling calmer, he went over to the eagle owl's den, crouched down silently, then suddenly popped up at the little window and went,

woo-oo, woo-oo,
and the Grand Duke flew to the pedestal and looked into his eyes, and Azarías told it very proudly,

I've been on a tawny owl chase,
and the bird pricked up its ears and clicked its beak, as if to celebrate, and,

I gave it a good run for its money,
and he laughed quietly, hissing softly, feeling safe back in the farm compound, and so it went, time and again, year after year, until one night in early June, he went up to the bars of the window of the den and as usual went,

woo-oo, woo-oo!

but the Grand Duke didn't come, and Azarías was surprised, and said again,

woo-oo, woo-oo!

but the Grand Duke didn't come, and Azarías,

woo-oo, woo-oo!

insistently, a third time, but there was no sound, so holding his oil lamp, Azarías pushed open the door, only to discover the eagle owl shriveled up in a corner, and, when he offered it a magpie to eat, it didn't even twitch, so Azarías placed the magpie on the ground and sat down next to the eagle owl, gripped its wings tenderly, and cradled it in his warm bosom, scratching its brow hard and saying softly,

pretty kitey,

but the bird didn't respond to the usual enticements, so Azarías laid it on the straw and went out to look for the señorito,

kitey is sick, señorito, it's got a temperature,

he told him, and the señorito,

what can we do, Azarías! it's old, we need to find a new bird,

and Azarías, heartbroken,

but it's kitey, señorito,

and the señorito, his eyes half-closed,

aren't all birds the same?

and Azarías implored,

will the señorito please let me contact the Wise Man of Almendral?

and the señorito indolently leaned his left shoulder forward and said,

the Wise Man? too expensive, Azarías, we can't call the Wise Man for every sick bird, when would it end?

and after that reprimand, he cackled like the tawny owl, and that gave Azarías goose bumps, and,

señorito, don't laugh like that, I am begging you,
and the señorito,

I'm not allowed to laugh in my own house?
and he cackled again like the tawny owl, louder and louder, and his thunderous guffaws brought the señorita, Lupe, Dacio the Pigman, Dámaso and the shepherds' girls, and everybody else out into the hallway, all laughing like tawny owls, in a chorus, and Lupe,

I hope that little liar ain't crying over that stinking bird,
and Azarías,

kitey's got a temperature and the señorito won't let me
contact the Wise Man of Almendral,
and the laughter grew louder and louder until finally a distraught Azarías ran out into the big yard and peed on his hands and then went into the stable, sat on the ground, and started counting valve tops aloud, trying to calm himself down,

one, two, three, four, five, six, seven, eight, nine, ten,
eleven, forty-three, forty-four, forty-five,
until he felt a little better, and laying his head down on a sack, he took a siesta, and as soon as morning dawned, he quietly sidled up to the bars of the den and went,

woo-oo, woo-oo
but nobody replied, and Azarías pushed the door open and saw the eagle owl in the corner where he'd left it the night before, stiff on the ground, and Azarías tiptoed over, grasped the corner of one wing, and, opening his jacket, deposited the bird inside, and said in a wavering voice,

pretty kitey,
but the Grand Duke didn't open its eyes or click its beak or do anything at all, so Azarías crossed the big yard, he reached

the front gate and unbolted it, and when its hinges squeaked, Lupe, Dacio's wife, came out,

what's gotten into your head now, Azarías?

and Azarías,

I'm going to my sister's,

and with that, he left, walking so quickly he didn't even feel the pebbles or prickly cammock underfoot as he crossed the copse of holm oaks, the broom, and the riverbed, gently holding the bird's body against his chest, and the second Régula caught sight of him,

you're back?

and Azarías,

how are the boys?

and Régula,

they're at school,

and Azarías,

nobody's home?

and Régula,

Tiny is here,

and right then Régula noticed Azarías's bulging chest, and when she pulled at the ends of his jacket and the giant bird fell on the red tiles, Régula screamed hysterically,

you take that carcass out of my house right now, you hear me?

and after Azarías sheepishly picked up the bird and left it on the stone bench outside, he came back into the house and emerged with Tiny, cradling her in his right arm, and Tiny stared blankly, her eyes looking at nothing in particular, and Azarías picked up the bird by its leg with his right hand and a shovel with his left, and Régula,

where are you off to with that?

and Azarías,

to bury kitey,

and on their way, Tiny let out one of those endless piercing screams that could turn anyone's blood to ice, but Azarías didn't flinch, he reached the skirt of the hillside, placed the girl on the ground between a few rockroses, took off his jacket, and dug a deep hole by the bottom of a cork oak, put the bird inside, and, as soon as he had done so, covered the bird with soil, and once he'd filled the hole, he stood and looked at the mound, barefoot, trousers patched at the back of the knees, mouth agape, and after a while he looked at Tiny, whose head flopped loosely to one side, their blank eyes meeting before both gazed once more into empty space, and Azarías crouched down, took her in his arms, sat on the edge of the slope by the earth he'd stirred, pressed her against his chest, and whispered,

pretty kitey,

and he began scratching the hair above the nape of her neck hard with the index finger of his right hand, and Tiny let him.

Book Two
Shorty Paco

If they'd always lived on the Cortijo,* maybe things would have been different, but Crespo the Gamekeeper liked to send someone to keep an eye on the Abendújar boundary line just in case, and Shorty Paco, as they called him, got the short straw, not that it put him out personally, because at the end of the day, they had to make do with what they got, as far as he was concerned, but it did matter for the boys, that is, for their schooling, but they had enough on their plate with Charito, or Tiny, as they called her, though in truth she was the oldest, but they called her Tiny because she seemed like a baby,

mother, why can't Charito talk?

why can't Charito walk, mother?

why does Charito dirty her panties?

they asked every half hour, and Régula, or he, or both together,

---

*Translator's note: "Cortijos" were large farmsteads on the landed estates in Andalucía and Extremadura. These farmsteads included large houses for the wealthy owners and their administrator and, until the 1960s, hovels for the laborers near the animal sheds. This estate, like many in Extremadura, undoubtedly had "dehesas," or pastures for fighting bulls. Luis Buñuel's 1933 documentary *Las Hurdes* (*Land Without Bread*) shows the dire living conditions of peasants in Extremadura before the civil war.

because Charito is very young,
since they had to say something, what else could they tell them? but Shorty Paco wanted his kids to get an education, the Hashemite in Cordovilla assured them that their kids could escape poverty with just a bit of knowledge, and even the Señora Marquesa herself, hoping to eradicate illiteracy on the farmstead, brought two señoritos from the city three summers in a row, so when everyone had finished working, they all gathered at the entrance to the yard, the shepherds, the pigmen, the beaters, the muleteers, the cowhands and guards, and there, in the light of the oil lamps, with moths and bluebottles buzzing around, the señoritos taught them the letters of the alphabet and their thousands of mysterious combinations, and the shepherds, and the pigmen, and the beaters, and the cowhands, when asked, said,

B with A makes bah, and C with A makes sah,
and the señoritos from the city, Señorito Gabriel and Señorito Lucas, corrected them and explained all the traps, and told them,

no, sometimes, C with A makes kah, and C with E makes seh, and C with I makes sih, and C with O makes koh,
and the pigmen, and the shepherds, and the muleteers, and the cowhands, and the guards became frustrated and muttered to each other,

the things they say, I think they're making fun of us,
but they didn't dare speak out of turn until one night, after Shorty Paco had had a few drinks, he confronted the tall señorito, the one with the receding hairline, the leader of the group, and, flaring the nostrils of his broad nose (through which, according to Señorito Iván, on days when he was in a joking mood, you could catch a glimpse of his brains), he asked,

Señorito Lucas, what's the point of these games?
and Señorito Lucas burst out laughing, and laughed uncontrollably until he turned red, until finally, when he'd calmed down a bit, he wiped his eyes with a handkerchief and said,

it's grammar, ask the scholars why,
and he said no more, but of course, that was only the start, for one evening they got to H, and Señorito Lucas told them,

H with A makes hah, and H with E makes heh, but sometimes it also makes hee, like hee-hee,
and Shorty Paco lost his temper, that was too much shit, they were ignorant but they weren't stupid, and why the hell were E and I always exceptions to the rules, and Señorito Lucas burst into nervous laughter, and as usual, he said that he was just the messenger and those were the rules of grammar and he didn't make them, but if they felt cheated, they should write to the scholars, since his job was only to explain how grammar worked, not why the rules were what they were, but all this infuriated Shorty Paco, and his anger boiled over when one night Señorito Lucas drew a beautiful capital H on the blackboard, and after clapping loudly to call them to attention and shut them up, he warned,

be very careful with this letter; this letter is a special case, my friends; this letter can be silent,
and Shorty Paco thought to himself, well, it's just like Charito, because she never said anything at all, only now and then let out a pitiful moan that rocked the house to its foundations, but at this news from Señorito Lucas about the letter H, Facundo the Pigman crossed his arms over his paunch and said,

what do you mean it can be silent? if you think about it, the others only talk when we lend them our voice,
and Señorito Lucas, the tall fellow with the receding hairline,

sometimes it doesn't make a sound, I mean, it's as if it
didn't exist, it's a blank,
and Facundo the Pigman, keeping his abbot's stance,
a silent letter? then what's the point?
and Señorito Lucas,
it's a question of aesthetics,
he acknowledged,
it's only there to embellish words, to ensure that the vowel
that comes after doesn't feel abandoned, but even so, anyone who doesn't include it where it belongs makes a real
mistake—indeed, commits a crime against grammar
and Shorty Paco, completely at a loss, was even more con-
fused; the next morning he once again saddled up the mare
before going to patrol the perimeter, which was his job, but
ever since Señorito Lucas had started on about the letters of
the alphabet, he was a different man, he was always lost in
thought, couldn't think about anything else, and as soon as
he galloped away from the farmstead, he dismounted, sat in
the shadow of an arbutus, and turned it all over in his mind,
and when the grammatical rules got mixed up in his head,
he resorted to using pebbles to try to make sense of it all, the
white pebbles were E and I, and gray ones were A, O, and U,
and then he got mixed up trying to work out how the words
sounded, and he couldn't figure it out, and at night he con-
fided his doubts to Régula, on their straw bed, and, imperceptibly, one thing led to another, and Régula,
stop it, Paco, Rogelio's tossing and turning,
and when Paco persisted, she,
hey, stop, I don't feel like it,
and suddenly Tiny let out a searing cry, and Paco froze,
thinking something must be terribly wrong with him to have

fathered such a child, as silent as the letter H and as useless, and just as well that Nieves was so lively, that he'd resisted christening her with such a white, snowy name, it didn't fit, you know, he being so swarthy and dark, he'd have rather called her Herminia, like his grandma, or by any other name, but that summer a torrid sun had blistered down and Don Pedro the Administrator had harped on about the temperatures not going below ninety-five even at night, and what a summer, by God, nobody could remember anything like it, even the birds were frying, and Régula, who was flushed by nature, complained,

Mary Mother of God, it's hot! not even a breeze day or night,

and after wearily fanning herself with a palm-leaf fan, moving only the knuckle of her right thumb, the one that was squashed flat like a spatula, she added,

this must be some kind of punishment, Paco, I'm going to ask the Virgin of the Snows to let up,

but the dog days went on and on, and one Sunday, without telling a soul, she went to Almendral, where the Wise Man lived, and upon returning, she told Paco,

Paco, the Wise Man told me that if I'm pregnant with a girl, we have to name her Nieves, or else the child will have problems,

and Paco remembered Tiny and agreed,

all right, let's call her Nieves,

but Nieves, who, as a youngster cleaned up Tiny's messes and washed her clothes, didn't in the end go to the Foundation School, because by that time they were already living in Abendújar, and every morning Shorty Paco, before saddling up, taught Nieves how B went with A, and C with A, and C with I, and the young girl, who was very smart, soon neared the end of the alphabet, and he told her,

S and I make sih,

she replied right away,

you don't really need the letter S, dad, C and I can also make sih,

and Shorty Paco laughed and, imitating Señorito Lucas, said,

tell that to the scholars,

and at night, feeling content, he'd say to Régula,

that girl is so clever,

and Régula, whose bust had filled out over recent months, commented,

she has more than enough talent for herself and the other girl,

and Paco,

what other girl?

and Régula, as matter-of-fact as usual,

Tiny, of course, who else would I be talking about?

and Paco,

why don't you show me your talent,

and he started to touch her, and she,

stop it, Paco, there's a lack of talent down there right now,

and Shorty Paco egged her on, enjoying every second of it, until unexpectedly, a roar from Tiny rent the silence of the night, and Paco grew still, went soft, and finally said,

God be with you, Régula, sleep tight,

and over the years, he got used to Abendújar and the white-washed hovel with its vine, the small outhouse and the well and the huge cork oak giving shade to everything, and the bevy of gray boulders scattered over the expanse of land, and the tepid stream with the turtles lazing on its banks, but one October morning, Shorty Paco stepped out the door, but this time he looked up and flared his nostrils,

a horse is coming,

he said, and beside him Régula shaded her eyes with her right hand and looked toward the road,

I don't see a soul, Paco,

but Shorty Paco sniffed the air like a bloodhound, and he added,

it's Crespo, if I'm not mistaken,

because Shorty Paco's sense of smell was keener than any pointer's, according to Señorito Iván; he could detect something far, far away, and, true enough, within a few minutes, Crespo the Gamekeeper rode into Abendújar,

Paco, pack your bags, you're back on the Cortijo,

he told him, and Paco,

why on earth?

and Crespo,

orders from Don Pedro the Administrator, Lucio will be here at midday, you've done your stint here,

and later, in the cool of the day, Paco and Régula piled their belongings on the cart and made their way back, the children perched comfortably on top of the mattresses and, at the back, Régula with the screaming Tiny, whose head flopped from side to side, her thin, inert legs peeking out from under her housecoat, and Shorty Paco, riding on his piebald mare, escorted them all, proudly bringing up the rear, and, raising his voice in order to be heard over the thud-thud-thud of the wheels in the ruts and Tiny's screams, he yelled to Régula,

now Nieves can go to school and she'll go far, she's so smart, and Régula,

    we'll see about that,

and from his majestic height, Shorty Paco added,

    the boys are old enough to work now, they'll help us
    make ends meet,

and Régula,

    we'll see about that,

and Paco went on, excited by the noise and this new chapter,

    the new house will probably have an extra room and we
    can be young again,

and Régula sighed, cradled Tiny, and swatted away the mosquitos while above the path, over the black holm oaks, the stars lit up one by one, and Régula looked up, sighed again, and said,

    for us to be young again, this little one would have to stay
    quiet,

and once they reached the Cortijo, Crespo the Gamekeeper was waiting for them by the old house, the one they'd left five years before, with the long stone bench by the door and the wilting geraniums lining the walls, and, in the middle of the yard, the willow offering warm shade, and a glum Paco took it all in, shook his head from side to side, and then looked down,

    what can we do!

he said, resigned,

    it must be God's will,

and Don Pedro the Administrator was in front of them, shouting orders, and

    good evening, Don Pedro, here we are again,

    may God bless us, Paco, all is well in Abendújar?

and Paco,

all is well, Don Pedro,
and as they unloaded, Don Pedro trailed them from the cart
to the door and from the door to the cart,
     Régula, you will look after the front gate like you used to,
     and unbolt it the second you hear the car, you know how
     the señora and Señorito Iván don't like to be kept waiting,
and Régula,
     Don Pedro, your wish is our command,
and Don Pedro,
     tomorrow you'll let out the turkeys and clean out the
     coops, otherwise nobody can stand the smell, it's such a
     stink, and you know the señora is understanding but she
     likes things to be spick and span,
and Régula,
     Don Pedro, your wish is our command,
and Don Pedro the Administrator went on giving orders,
never stopped giving orders, and when he finally did stop,
he leaned his head to one side, chewed his left cheek, and
looked uneasy, as if he'd forgotten something very important, and Régula, meekly,
     anything else, Don Pedro?
and Don Pedro the Administrator chewed his cheek and
glanced at Nieves but said nothing, and, finally, when it
seemed he'd leave without saying a word, he suddenly turned
toward Régula,
     there *is* something else, Régula,
he stammered,
     it's really women's business, but . . .
and the pause went on and on, until Régula, meekly,
     out with it, Don Pedro,
and Don Pedro,

it's about your girl, Régula, your girl could give my señora a hand in the house; as you know, she's not so keen on housework,

he smiled sourly,

I mean, cleaning just isn't her strong suit, and your girl's grown up so much, it's amazing what a spurt she's had,

and, as Don Pedro was talking, Shorty Paco deflated like a balloon, like his manliness deep in the night when Tiny screamed, and he looked at Régula, and Régula looked at him, and finally, Shorty Paco flared his nostrils, shrugged his shoulders, and said,

whatever you say, Don Pedro, we're here to serve,

and suddenly, out of the blue, Don Pedro the Administrator's eyes dilated, and he began to ramble on, as if he were trying to bury something beneath an avalanche of words,

now everyone wants to be a señorito, Paco, you know, things aren't what they used to be; nowadays nobody wants to get their hands dirty, and some are off to the capital and others to foreign places, whatever; the fact is it only gets worse and worse, it's the way the world is going, people think they're going to solve all these problems; just imagine, then it turns out that maybe they'll go hungry or be bored to death, God knows, but your girl will never go without in the house, and not just because I say so . . .

and Régula and Shorty Paco nodded and exchanged knowing glances, but Don Pedro the Administrator didn't notice, for he was very agitated,

and if you agree, we'll expect your girl in the house tomorrow morning, and so you don't miss her, and she doesn't get herself into trouble, we know what young people are like nowadays, she can sleep here at night, and after lots of arm-waving and gesticulating, Don Pedro departed, and Régula and Shorty Paco silently began to sort their belongings, and then they ate supper, and after supper they sat by the fireside, and just then, Facundo the Pigman burst in,

you've got balls, Paco, not even God could stay up there in the Casa de Arriba, you know what Doña Purita's like, acting like someone's sticking pins into her all the time, she gets so hysterical, not even *he* can stand her,

but as neither Régula nor Shorty Paco responded, Facundo quickly added,

well, you don't know her, Paco, if you don't believe me, ask Pepa, because she's worked there,

but Régula and Paco said nothing, so Facundo the Pigman turned around and left, and in the morning, Nieves went to the Casa de Arriba as ordered, and the next day too, until it became routine, and the days went by without anyone noticing, until one day in May, Carlos Alberto, Señorito Iván's eldest son, showed up for his First Communion in the Cortijo chapel, and two days later, after everybody had been running around, the Marquesa arrived with the bishop in the big car, and the second Régula opened the front gate, she was dazzled by the purple of his robes, and, flustered and unsure what to do, she bowed her head twice, genuflected, and crossed herself, but from above the Marquesa prompted her,

the ring, Régula, the ring,

and Régula smothered the pastoral ring in kisses, and the bishop smiled before discreetly removing his hand, and, embarrassed, he strode across the yard into the Casa Grande, past bowing pigmen and farmhands, and the next day there was a big party, and after the religious ceremony in the small chapel, all the laborers gathered in the big yard for hot chocolate and fried breadcrumb hash and,

long live Señorito Carlos Alberto!

and,

long live the señora!

they rejoiced, but Nieves couldn't be there because she was serving the guests in the Casa Grande, which she did with much aplomb, removing dirty plates with her left hand and replacing them with her right, and when it was time to pass around the giant platters of food, she gently leaned over the guest's left shoulder, her right forearm behind her back, smiling serenely and showing such discretion that the señora noticed and asked Don Pedro the Administrator where he'd found that jewel of a girl, and Don Pedro the Administrator, surprised,

she's the guard Shorty Pacos's, Iván's hunting attendant, the guy who was working in Abendújar until a few months ago, she's his younger girl who's suddenly grown up,

and the señora,

Régula's?

and Don Pedro the Administrator,

that's right, Régula's, Purita brought her up to speed in a month, that girl's smart,

and the señora couldn't take her eyes off Nieves, tracking her every movement, at one point remarking to her daughter,

have you seen that girl? how she carries herself! a bit more polishing and she'd make a good first maid,

and Señorita Miriam, watching Nieves out of the corner of her eye,

she isn't bad at all,

she said,

but too big up here for my liking

she said, pointing to her bosom, but Nieves, though she felt somewhat flustered, was transfigured by the presence of the little boy, Carlos Alberto, he was so fair and lovely in his white sailor suit, with his white rosary and white missal, and as she served him, she couldn't help but beam at him as if smiling at an angel, and that night, the moment she was back home, though worn out by the day's excitement, she told Shorty Paco firmly,

father, I want to take First Communion,

Shorty Paco was startled,

what are you saying?

and she, stubbornly,

that I want to take First Communion, father,

and Shorty Paco lifted both hands to his head as if to keep it from flying off his neck,

we'll have to talk to Don Pedro, love,

and when Don Pedro the Administrator heard about the girl's aspirations from Shorty Paco, he burst out laughing and threw up his hands,

who does she think she is, Paco? I mean, come on, taking First Communion? it's not a game, Paco, it's a deadly
serious matter,

and Shorty Paco bowed his head,

if you say so,

but Nieves was insistent, she wouldn't back down, and, given Don Pedro the Administrator's do-nothing attitude, she ap-pealed to Doña Purita,

señorita, I'm only fourteen, but I feel this longing deep
inside me,

and Doña Purita, quite taken aback, opened her bright red lips and said,

> what a crazy idea, love! sure it's not a man you're really after?

and she laughed until her sides hurt and repeated,

> what a crazy idea!

and from then on, Nieves's wish was regarded both in the Casa de Arriba and the Casa Grande as nonsense, and it became a favorite topic of gossip, and whenever Señorito Iván's guests came and the conversation was petering out for whatever reason, Doña Purita would point a pink manicured finger at Nieves and exclaim,

> look at that girl over there, she's got the crazy idea in her head that she wants to take Communion,

and there were shouts of astonishment and sidelong glances around the big table, as well as prolonged muttering, like the flutter of a bird's wings, and, in the corner, stifled laughter, and the second the girl left, Señorito Iván,

> this blasted Vatican Council is to blame,

and the odd guest stopped eating and stared at him, almost quizzically, and Señorito Iván felt duty bound to explain,

> it's the ideas they promote, they're saying they should be treated as people, and that's just ridiculous, you see that with your own eyes, but they're not to blame, the blasted Council is to blame for sowing unrest,

and at such moments, and other similar ones, Doña Purita half closed her languid eyes, thick with black mascara, turned toward Señorito Iván, and brushed the end of her snub nose against the lobe of his ear, and Señorito Iván leaned over and rakishly peered down her swooping neckline into her beautiful cleavage, and, to justify his action, added,

what do you think, Pura, you know them, don't you?
but Don Pedro the Administrator watched them from across
the way, chewing the inside of his thin cheek, and, at the end
of his rope, he lost it completely once the guests left and he
was alone with Doña Purita in the Casa de Arriba,

> you wear a half-cup bra and a plunging neckline when
> he's around to get him all worked up, or do you think I
> was born yesterday?

he stammered, and whenever they drove back from the city,
movies, or theater, you could hear him shouting the same
refrain before they got out of the car,

> whore, whore's too good a word for you!

but Doña Purita ignored him and hummed to herself, and after alighting from the car, she started pouting and dancing
on the entrance steps, swaying her hips and looking down at
her tiny feet as she said,

> why should I be ashamed that the Lord made me so
> attractive?

and Don Pedro the Administrator chased after her, his cheeks
bright red, his ears pale white,

> it's that you flaunt it shamelessly, you're a bigger specta-
> cle than any on stage,

he let fly, but Doña Purita never lost her composure, she
just walked down the long hallway, hands on hips, swaying
provocatively, singing to herself, and he slammed the door,
went over to the stand, and grabbed a riding whip,

> I'll teach you how to behave!

he roared, and she came to a halt in front of him, stopped
singing, and stared at him defiantly,

> you wouldn't dare, you chicken, but if you ever do touch
> me with that thing, you can kiss me goodbye,

she said, and she started sashaying again after she'd turned her back on him, making her way toward their bedroom, and he followed behind in a frenzy, waving his arms, but besides shouts, he emitted staccato howls, and at the height of his tantrum, his voice broke, he threw the whip onto a piece of furniture, burst out sobbing, and whined,

you enjoy making me suffer, Pura, I only do what I do because I love you,

but Doña Purita started pouting and sashaying once again,

now you're making a scene again,

she said, and to distract herself she stood in front of the large wardrobe mirror and struck a few poses, admiring herself, head tilted back, tossing her hair, smiling more and more broadly until she strained the corners of her lips, while Don Pedro the Administrator collapsed facedown on the bed, hiding his face in his hands and crying like a child, and Nieves, who had witnessed most of his performance, gathered her things together and walked slowly back home, and, if by chance Shorty Paco was awake, she'd say,

they had a serious fight tonight, father, he called her everything under the sun,

and Shorty Paco, incredulous,

Don Pedro?

and he lifted both hands to his head, as if it were about to fly off and he needed to hold it down, and said calmly,

these arguments in the Casa de Arriba are none of your business, my love, you just watch, listen, and keep quiet,

but the day after one such ruckus, it was the biggest hunt of the year on the Cortijo, All Saints' Day, and Don Pedro the Administrator, who was a mediocre shot, didn't hit a single partridge despite there being so many, and Señorito Iván, in the adjacent blind, who'd just shot down four birds from the same covey, two at the front and two at the back, commented sarcastically to Shorty Paco,

I wouldn't believe it if I hadn't seen it with my own two eyes; when will that fag ever learn? they're practically begging him to shoot them, but he hasn't hit a single one, did you see, Paco?

Of course I did, Señorito Iván, you would have to be blind not to,

and the señorito,

he never was a great shot, but he misses too many for it to be normal, something's wrong with the idiot,

and Shorty Paco,

don't think so, hunting's a lottery, today's great, tomorrow's the pits, it is what it is,

and Señorito Iván hit the target time and again, reacting remarkably quickly, and between one bang-bang and the next, he'd quip, twisting his mouth against the butt of his gun,

a lottery up to a point, Paco, but let's be clear, the way the birds are coming at that fag, you could catch them with your cap,

and that afternoon, at the lunch in the Casa Grande, Doña Purita showed up again with the half-cup bra and plunging neckline and came on to Señorito Iván, all winks and smiles, while Don Pedro the Administrator simmered at the far end of the table, feeling helpless, nibbling his thin cheek, and shaking so violently he couldn't use his knife and fork, and when Doña Purita leaned her head on Señorito Iván's shoulder and they began to stroke one another, Don Pedro the Administrator half stood up, raised his arm, wagged a finger, and roared, trying to distract everyone,

look, that girl over there is desperate to take First
Communion!

and Nieves, who was removing plates at that point, felt her
stomach turn, and she blushed and stumbled but smiled
pleasantly enough, although Don Pedro the Administrator was still waving an accusing finger implacably at her,
shouting like a lunatic, beside himself, while everyone else
laughed,

why are you turning so red, my girl? don't smash the
plates!

until Señorita Miriam took pity on Nieves and jumped in,
and why shouldn't she?

and Don Pedro the Administrator, calmer now, lowered his
head and mumbled, hardly moving his lips,

Miriam, this girl knows absolutely nothing about anything, and her father is poorer than a pig, so how could
she ever take First Communion properly?

and Señorita Miriam craned her neck, lifted her head, and
asked, as if in a state of shock,

and is there nobody in this entire gathering who could
lend her a helping hand?

and she stared at Doña Purita on the other side of the table,
but Don Pedro the Administrator had shut up, and that night
in the Casa de Arriba, he asked Nieves, almost offhandedly,

you're not angry with me, I hope, because of what happened this afternoon, are you, girl? I was only joking,

but his mind was elsewhere, because while he was talking
to Nieves, he was walking over to Doña Purita, and when he
reached her, his eyes narrowed, his face tight, he grasped her
bare, fragile shoulders with his trembling hands and said,

care to share what you're playing at?

but Doña Purita scornfully shook him off, turned away, and started pouting and singing, and Don Pedro the Administrator, beside himself, grabbed the riding crop from the stand again and went after her,

I'm not going to forgive you this time, you little whore! he bawled, and he was so livid his words stuck in his throat, but a few minutes after he'd walked into the bedroom, Nieves heard him collapse on the bed and start whimpering into his pillow as usual.

Book Three
Kitey

Around this time Azarías turned up at the Cortijo, and Régula welcomed him and laid out a sack of straw for him by the kitchen as she always did, but Azarías didn't even look at her, he muttered and worked his jaw up and down as if he were chewing something, and his sister,

what's wrong, Azarías, are you sick?
but Azarías just stared blankly at the fire, growled, and clenched his toothless gums, and Régula,

don't tell me another of your pretty birdies has died, Azarías,
and after some time, Azarías,

the señorito fired me, he says I'm too old,
and Régula,

well, the señorito can't do that if you've gotten old working for him,
and Azarías,

I'm only a year older than the señorito,
and he mumbled and chewed, perched on the stool, elbows on his thighs, head between his hands, staring blankly at the hearth, and then out of the blue Tiny shrieked, and Azarías's eyes lit up and his lips broadened into a wet smile, and he said to his sister,

let me see Tiny,
and Régula,

  she's probably dirty,
and Azarías,

  go get her,
and, since he insisted, Régula got up and came back with
Charito, whose body was as small as a rabbit's, her little legs
dangling and flopping like a rag doll's, as if she didn't have
any bones, but Azarías's trembling hands cradled her head
in his lap, he gently held her in his brawny arms, holding
her to his chest, and he began softly scratching her brow
while he whispered,

  pretty kitey, pretty kitey . . .
and as soon as Shorty Paco was back from his afternoon patrol around the perimeter, Régula went out to meet him,

  hey, Paco, we've got a visitor, guess who it is,
and Shorty Paco sniffed the air for a second and said,

  it's your brother,
and she,

    that's right, but not for a night or two this time, for this
    time he's here to stay, he says the señorito fired him, I
    don't get it, we'll have to find out what happened,
and the following morning, at the crack of dawn, Shorty
Paco saddled the mare and galloped off, across the ford and
the countryside full of scrub and rockroses, and turned up at
the señorito's farmstead, trailed by howling mastiffs, but the
señorito was resting, so Shorty Paco dismounted and started
to shoot the breeze with Lupe, wife of Dacio the Pigman,

    he's covered in fleas, he smells like shit, and as if that
    weren't bad enough, he pees on his hands, the man has
    no shame—

and Shorty Paco nodded, but,

    what else is new, Lupe?

and Lupe,

    well, it's nothing new, but at the end of the day, it gets
    you down,

and she went on with her litany of complaints until the señorito appeared, and then Shorty Paco stood up, as he was ex-
pected to do, and the señorito,

    good morning,

    may the Lord make it so, señorito,

and Shorty Paco took his cap off and started turning it over
in his hands, as if it were in the way, and, finally,

    señorito, Azarías says you fired him, how can this be pos-
    sible after all these years?

the señorito,

    let's get this straight, who do you think you are? who gave
    you any right to butt in?

and Shorty Paco, shifting on his heels,

    I'm sorry, I'm Azarías's brother-in-law, from Pilón, the
    Marquesa's place, a farmhand employed by Crespo the
    Gamekeeper, if that makes sense,

and Azarías's señorito,

    ah, I know you!

and he nodded slowly, eyes shut, as if he was thinking, and,
finally, he concurred,

    well, Azarías isn't lying, it's true that I fired him, I mean,
    a fellow who pees on his hands, I can't eat a woodcock
    he's plucked, don't you see? with hands he's pissed on! it's
    disgusting, and if he can't pluck my woodcocks, what else
    does an old crock like him do on the farm, especially one
    who doesn't have anything going on up here?

and he pointed to his forehead, jabbing his finger against his temple, and Shorty Paco looked at the toes of his boots and kept twirling his cap as he listened to the rant, and finally he plucked up his courage, and,

> no doubt, you're quite within your rights, señorito, but just think for a sec, my brother-in-law has spent his whole life here, he'll be sixty-one come Saint Eutychius Day, and that's a big slice of life, you know . . .

but the señorito waved a hand and interrupted him,

> that's all very well, but don't you go raising your voice at me, I deserve a medal for putting up with your brother-in-law for sixty-one years, do you hear me? this is a fine time to be giving charity to an imbecile who shits all over the place and, to make matters worse, pees on his hands before plucking my woodcocks, I mean, it's completely disgusting,

and Shorty Paco, still twirling his cap, nodded ever more slightly,

> I'll look after him, señorito, but, I mean, we only have two rooms and four kids, we're on top of each other . . .

and the señorito,

> that's all very well, but I'm not running a charity, and that's what families are for, don't you agree?

and Shorty Paco,

> I guess so,

and he slowly walked back to his mare, but when he put his foot in the stirrup and mounted, the señorito called after him,

> oh, and Azarías swears and takes the valve tops from my friends' car tires, just imagine, even the Minister's; you must understand I can't invite anyone over anymore . . .

and his voice got louder and louder as Shorty Paco cantered off on the mare . . .

their tires go completely flat . . . you must understand! but, of course, Azarías *was* a bother, like Tiny, as Régula said, innocents, a couple of little innocents, but even Charito shut up now and then, but Azarías rambled on from dawn to dusk, and at night he never even slept, just walked around coughing, and he'd start whining like a dog till sunrise, when he'd peer into the yard, dribbling, his pants around his knees, and the pigmen and the guards and the farmhands always offered the same refrain,

going fishing, Azarías? and he'd smile into empty space as he cleaned out the coops and moaned between clenched gums, and when he'd finished, he'd grab a bucket in each hand and say,

I'm off to get manure for the flowers, and he'd go through the front gate and disappear up the hillside, between the rockroses and the holm oaks, looking for Antonio Abad the Shepherd, who couldn't be far away at that time of day, and as soon as he found him, he'd start walking slowly behind his flock, crouching down and collecting fresh droppings until he'd filled his buckets, and then he'd walk back to the Cortijo whispering inaudibly, dried spit caking the corners of his mouth, and as soon as he was in the yard, Pepa would already be there, or Abundio, or Remedios, Crespo's wife, or whoever,

Azarías is back with the manure for the geraniums, and Azarías would smile and walk along the edge of the flowerbeds and flowerpots, distributing the manure evenly, and Pepa, or Abundio, or Remedios, or even Crespo himself,

he brings more shit into the farm than he takes out,

and Régula, patiently,

hey, he's not bothering anyone, at least it keeps him busy,
but Facundo, or Remedios, or Pepa, or even Crespo would
scowl,

you'll see what the señora says when she comes,
but Azarías was hard-working and methodical, and morning after morning he came back from the holm oaks with
two buckets of sheep droppings, and within a few weeks the
flowers in the beds pointed up from small conical mounds
of pellets, black as volcanoes, and Régula had to put her foot
down,

Azarías, that's enough manure, why don't you take Tiny
for a walk,

she told him, and at night she asked Shorty Paco to find
some other chores for Azarías, since the flowerbeds had
more than enough manure, and if he didn't have a job, he'd
become lethargic and sleep among the arbutus, and nobody
could stir him back to life, but around that time, Rogelio
their son worked alone, driving the tractor all around the
property, a brand-new red imported tractor, and he was so
handy with repairs that whenever he noticed Régula worry-
ing about Azarías, he'd say,

I'll take Azarías with me, mother,
because Rogelio was warm and talkative, quite unlike their
other son, Quirce, who became more taciturn and unsocia-
ble by the day, and Régula wondered,

what's been going on with Quirce lately?
but Quirce didn't say a word, and whenever he had a couple
of free hours, he disappeared from the Cortijo and returned
at night tipsy and gloomy, never smiling, never ever, except
when his brother Rogelio urged Azarías on,

uncle, why don't you count the corncobs?
and docile Azarías, desperate to oblige, went over to the enormous pile next to the silo, and
one, two, three, four, five . . .
he counted patiently, and, as always, when he reached eleven, he'd say,
forty-three, forty-four, forty-five,
and then and only then did Quirce break into a tight, forced smile, but Régula, his mother, bristled and scolded him, legs planted and arms waving wildly, her eyes accusing,
hey, that's not nice, mocking an old innocent is an insult to God,
and all in a huff she went off to find Tiny, took her in her arms, and gave her to Azarías,
here you are, get her to sleep, she's the only one who understands you,
and Azarías cradled Tiny lovingly, and sitting on the stone bench by the door, he rocked her and kept repeating in that thick, garbled voice of his,
pretty kitey, pretty kitey,
until they fell asleep together in the half light under the vine, smiles on both their faces, but, one morning, when Régula was combing Tiny's hair, she found a flea between the teeth of the comb, saw red, and went over to where Azarías was,
Azarías, when was the last time you took a bath?
only señoritos take baths,
and Régula,
señoritos my ass, water is free, you filthy pig,
and Azarías silently showed her both sides of his hands, dirt in every wrinkle, and finally said humbly by way of explanation,

I pee on them every morning so they don't chap,
and Régula, beside herself,

you're such a pig, can't you see you're passing your nasty
germs on to Tiny?

but Azarías just looked at her plaintively with his yellow eyes,
then he hung his head, moaning and grinding his gums together, and his meekness and innocence disarmed his sister,

you lazy good-for-nothing, I have to watch you like a
baby,

and the following afternoon, she clambered onto the trailer
next to Rogelio and went to the Hashemite's store in Cordovilla, bought three T-shirts, and, back home, marched up to
Azarías,

you put one on every week, do you hear?

and Azarías nodded and grimaced, but after a month, Régula caught up with him by the willow,

what did you do with the T-shirts I bought you? It's been
four weeks and I haven't washed one,

and Azarías lowered his yellowy, bloodshot eyes and mumbled imperceptibly until his sister lost patience, grabbed his
arms, and shook him from side to side, and she found the
three T-shirts, layered one on top of the other,

you pig, you filthy little pig, take them all off at once, do
you hear me?

and Azarías meekly took off his patched brown corduroy
jacket and then the T-shirts, one by one, and bared his mus-
cular torso covered in gray-white hair, and Régula,

when you take one off, you put on another, the clean one,

take off, put on, that's all there is to it,

and Rogelio started giggling and clapped his big tanned hand
over his mouth to stifle his laughter so as not to annoy his

mother, and Shorty Paco, sitting on the stone bench, watched the scene sorrowfully and, in the end, lowered his head,

he's worse than Tiny,

he whispered, and after some time, when spring came, Azarías began to hallucinate, and at all hours he'd see his brother, Ireneo, in black and white by night, and if he was lying in the flax fields in the daytime, Ireneo would appear to him in polychrome, big and almighty against the blue sky, like an image of God the Father on an engraving he'd once seen, and when that happened, Azarías got up and went to find Régula,

Ireneo came back today, Régula,

he'd say, and she,

not again, let poor Ireneo rest in peace,

and Azarías,

he's in heaven,

and she,

well, did he ever hurt anyone?

but Azarías's sayings immediately spread around the Cortijo, and the pigmen, shepherds, and farmhands made a point of running into him, and they'd ask,

what happened to Ireneo, Azarías?

and Azarías would shrug his shoulders,

he died, Franco sent him to heaven,

and they, as if it were the first time they'd ever asked,

and when was that, Azarías, when was that?

and Azarías would move his lips silently before replying,

a long time ago, when the Moors were here,

and they'd elbow each other and stifle their laughter and reply,

and are you sure Franco sent him to heaven? wouldn't he have sent him to hell?

and Azarías shook his head hard, dribbling and smiling, and pointed high into the blue,

I see him up there whenever I lie down in the flax fields, he said, but what was even worse for Shorty Paco was Azarías's habit of relieving himself, since at any hour of the day or night his brother-in-law would leave the house and look for a spot by the wall, or in the flowerbeds, or in the arbor, or by the willow to drop his pants, and every morning before Shorty Paco began his perimeter rounds, he first went out into the yard armed with a hoe like a gravedigger and tried to remove the traces before going back inside to Régula and lamenting,

the man must have an extremely loose sphincter, there's no other explanation,

and every day there was a fresh load, and out came Paco with his hoe to deal with it, but despite his best efforts, whenever he left the house, he couldn't help but flare his nostrils—through which, according to Señorito Iván, on days when he was in a joking mood, you could catch a glimpse of his brains—and wham! the stench hit him and he despaired,

can you smell that, Régula? it's a lost cause!

and Régula, downcast,

what do you expect me to do? we got the short end of the stick,

but around that time, Azarías began to miss chasing after the tawny owl, and whenever he caught his brother-in-law in a free moment, he said *Paco,* and Shorty Paco said nothing, as if he weren't there, and Azarías sweet-talked him,

take me to the mountains to chase after the tawny owl, Paco,

and Shorty Paco did not respond until one afternoon, out of
the blue, he had a bright idea, and he cheerfully turned to
his brother-in-law,

if I take you to the mountains, will you do it in the undergrowth and stop taking dumps in the yard?

and Azarías,

if you say so,

and every night from then on, Shorty Paco hoisted Azarías
onto the rump of his mare and rode with him bareback, and
in the pitch-black night, they dismounted at the foot of the
mountain, and while Shorty Paco waited by the flat-topped
cork oak, Azarías disappeared into the thickets between the
rockroses and the scrub and, doubled over, fought his way
through the undergrowth like an animal in search of prey,
and after a long pause, Shorty Paco heard his shrill cry,

hey! hey!

and immediately after, silence, and then Azarías's vaguely
nasal voice again,

hey! hey!

and after three or four cries, the tawny owl replied,

hoo, hoo!

at which point Azarías burst into a run, grunting furiously,
and the tawny owl hooted behind him and now and then let
out a gloomy cackle, and Shorty Paco, from the stony ground
near the cork oak, heard the bracken snapping and the
tawny owl hooting and then its shattering guffaw and then
silence, and a quarter of an hour later, Azarías appeared,
face and hands covered in scratches, his face lit up in a dribbling smile,

I gave it a good run for its money, Paco,

and Shorty Paco reminded him,

did you also do your business?

and Azarías,

not yet, Paco, I didn't have time,

and Shorty Paco,

well, get a move on,

and Azarías, still smiling, licking the scratches on his hands, moved a few yards away, crouched down by a buckthorn, and took a dump, and so it went, day after day, until one afternoon at the end of May, Rogelio came to the house holding a baby jackdaw,

uncle, look what I brought you!

and everyone came out of the house, and when Azarías saw the defenseless bird, his eyes filled with tears, he took it carefully in his hands, and he whispered,

pretty kitey, pretty kitey,

and soothing it, he walked into the house, put it in a basket, and went out to look for material to build a nest, and that evening he asked Quirce for a sack of meal, and, mixing it with water in a rusty can, he stuck a dollop under the bird's beak and said in a soft voice,

tchak, tchak, tchak

and the little jackdaw trembled in the straw,

tchak, tchak, tchak

and every time the jackdaw opened its beak, Azarías stuffed a bit of meal into its maw with his dirty forefinger, one bite after another, and the bird swallowed it, and then one more bite after another, until the bird was full, quiet, and calm, but half an hour after it had finished its first meal, it demanded more, so Azarías repeated the operation, muttering softly,

pretty kitey,
his words barely audible, but Régula watched him and whispered into Rogelio's ear,
that's better, that was such a good idea,
and Azarías didn't forget the bird night or day, and when the first rays of sun appeared in the morning, he ran happily around the yard, from door to door, a silly smile dancing on his lips, his yellow eyes dilated,
pretty kitey is growing feathers,
he repeated, and everyone congratulated him or asked after Ireneo, except his nephew Quirce, who glared at him and asked,
why would you bring a pest like that into the house, uncle?
and Azarías looked at him in astonishment,
it's not a pest, it's kitey,
but Quirce shook his head indignantly and then spat out,
the hell it is! it's a black bird, and nothing good comes from black birds,
and Azarías looked at him in consternation for a moment, then looked lovingly at the box and forgot all about Quirce,
tomorrow I'll get it a worm,
he said, and the next morning, he started digging heartily in the middle flowerbed until he found a worm, and he took it between two fingers and gave it to the jackdaw, and the jackdaw swallowed with such gusto that Azarías chattered contentedly,
did you see that, Charito? she's a good girl, and tomorrow I'll look for another worm,
and bit by bit, the jackdaw got bigger and grew thick feathers, so now whenever Shorty Paco took Azarías out to chase the tawny owl, Azarías fretted impatiently,

hurry up, Paco, pretty kitey is expecting me,
and Shorty Paco,

did you do your business?
and Azarías,

pretty kitey is expecting me, Paco,
and Shorty Paco, relentlessly,

if you don't do your business, I'll keep you here all night
and kitey can starve to death,
and Azarías pulled down his pants,

you mustn't do that,
he mumbled, as he crouched next to a dwarf oak and
dropped his load, but he stood up before he had finished,

come on, Paco, quick,
and he hastily pulled up his pants,

kitey is expecting me,
and he puckered his lips in a wet smile and ground his gums
with relish, and this routine was repeated every day until
one morning, three weeks later, as he was walking around
the yard with the jackdaw on his forearm, it fluttered its
wings briefly and then shot to the top of the willow tree in a
flurry, and when he saw it sitting there, out of his reach for
the very first time, Azarías whimpered,

kitey got away, Régula,
and Régula looked out,

let it fly, God gave it wings,
but Azarías,

I don't want kitey to leave, Régula,
and in great distress he looked up anxiously at the top of the
willow tree, and the jackdaw's watery eyes darted this way
and that, taking in new sights, and then it turned its head

to peck the fleas off its back, and Azarías, infusing his voice with as much sweetness and love as he could possibly muster,

pretty kitey, pretty kitey,

ever so tenderly, but the bird didn't respond, and Régula leaned a small ladder against the tree, hoping to retrieve it, but she hadn't climbed up two steps before the jackdaw opened its wings, fluttered them a few times, and finally left the branch, and it clumsily, hesitantly, flew to the top of the chapel roof and perched on the belfry's weather vane, high above, and as Azarías looked at it, big teardrops welled in his eyes, as if scolding it for its attitude,

you weren't happy with me,

he said, and at that very moment, Críspulo arrived, followed by Rogelio, and Pepa, and Facundo, and Crespo, and the whole troop looked up at the weather vane, and the jackdaw swayed awkwardly, and Rogelio laughed,

when you raise crows, uncle . . .

and Facundo,

you know, they like their freedom,

and Régula insisted,

God gave them wings to fly,

and big teardrops rolled down Azarías's cheeks, and he slapped his face trying to scare them away and resumed his refrain,

pretty kitey, pretty kitey,

and he moved away from the group, all crowded together in the warm shade of the willow tree, and as he spoke his eyes never left the weather vane, until finally he was alone in the middle of the big yard in the blistering July sun, grimacing and waving his arms, his own shadow like a black ball at his feet, until suddenly he looked up, softened his tone, and shouted,

tchak!

and up on the weather vane, the jackdaw rocked back and forth, surveying the yard, and then it was still, and Azarías, observing its every movement, repeated,

tchak!

and the jackdaw stretched its neck and watched him, relaxed, then stretched its neck again, and Azarías repeated furiously,

tchak!!!

and suddenly, out of nowhere, as if some sort of electric current had passed between them, the bird perched on the arrow of the weather vane and began to screech frantically,

tchak! tchak! tchak!

and the onlookers standing in the shade of the willow fell silent, and all of a sudden the bird took flight, swooped down, and, before their astonished eyes, circled the perimeter of the yard three times before finally alighting on Azarías's right shoulder, where it pecked the nape of his neck as if to delouse it, and the motionless Azarías smiled, then turned his head slightly toward it and whispered, prayerlike,

pretty kitey, pretty kitey.

Book Four
The Hunting Attendant

In the middle of June, Quirce began to take the flock of merino ewes out every afternoon, and at sunset, the delicate music of his harmonica floated through the air from the direction of the sierra, while his brother Rogelio never stopped driving the tractor or Jeep up and down, always on the go,

this carburetor is misfiring,

the gear lever is stuck,

and so on, and Señorito Iván didn't seem to care, but whenever he visited the Cortijo, he watched the two of them, Quirce and Rogelio, and summoning Crespo to one side, he told him in confidence,

Crespo, keep an eye on those boys, for Shorty Paco is getting old, and I'll always need a hunting attendant,

but neither Quirce nor Rogelio had their father's sense of smell, for Paco was an exceptional case, good God! since he was a little boy—this was no mean feat—when they let loose a partridge with clipped wings into the scrub, Paco would follow its scent, crawling with his wide nose to the ground like a setter tracking its prey, and later on, he could even tell old tracks from new, he could distinguish the trace scents of male from female, and Señorito Iván, astonished, screwed up his green eyes and asked,

what does game smell like, Paco, you fag?

and Shorty Paco,

    you really can't smell anything, señorito?

and Señorito Iván,

    if I could, I wouldn't have asked,

and Shorty Paco,

    the things Señorito Iván gets into his head!

and also when Señorito Iván was a child,

    what does game smell like, Paco?

and Shorty Paco, solicitously,

    can you really not smell anything?

and little Iván,

    I can't, cross my heart and hope to die, I can't detect the
    smell of game one little bit,

and Paco,

    you'll learn, buddy, you'll see when you're older,

because Shorty Paco didn't understand his own talent until he saw that nobody else could do what he did, thus his conversations with Iván, for at a young age the boy started hunting grouse in the pond or the mudflats, quail in August in the stubble, turtledoves, wheeling back among the holm oaks, in September, partridges in October in fields and foothills, wild pigeons in February in Lucio del Teatino, and, in between, bigger game, chamois and deer, always with a rifle or a sporting gun, always bang-bang, bang-bang, bang-bang,

    this boy's really something,

said the señora, and night and day, in winter or summer, stalking, jumping through the brush, or beating, bang-bang, bang-bang, bang-bang, little Iván was never without his rifle or sporting gun in the scrub or near the ponds, and in 1943, in the starting shoot on the Day of the Race, to everyone's surprise, Iván, at only thirteen years of age, was in the top three, he had shot only eight birds fewer than Teba, such a thing had never been seen before, there were moments when he shot so fast that he had four dead birds in the air at the same time, all of it beggared belief, absolutely incredible, the little kid masterfully rubbing shoulders with the best guns from Madrid, and from that day forward, Iván wanted Shorty Paco with him, to put his nose and energy to good use, and he helped him finesse his skills since Shorty Paco wasn't great at reloading, so one day young Iván gave him two cartridges and an old gun and told him,

> every night, before you get into bed, you will load and unload the cartridges down the barrels a hundred times, Paco, until you're exhausted,

and added, after a pause,

> if you get to be the fastest loader and unloader, between that and your smell and memory, you'll be the best hunting attendant in the world, believe me,

and every night, before getting into bed, Shorty Paco dutifully opened and shut the gun, loading and unloading the cartridges through the barrels, and Régula,

> are you crazy, Paco?

and Shorty Paco,

> Iván says if I do this, I'll be the best,

and, after a month,

> Iván, I can load and unload the cartridges in no time,

and Iván,

> I'll believe it when I see it, Paco, don't be crass,

and after Paco showed the young man how skilled he was,

> that's it, Paco, keep practicing, keep it up,

said Iván after that demonstration, and things continued in this manner, Iván here, Iván there, and Paco didn't notice how the years were passing him by until one morning in the blind, the inevitable finally came to pass, after Shorty Paco said with all the goodwill in the world,

Iván, careful, aim right,

and Iván steadied himself silently, took aim, and, in a flash, hit two partridges in front of him and two behind him, and the first hadn't even hit the ground before he spun around to face Paco and said haughtily,

from now on, Paco, you will address me as Señorito Iván, I'm not a child,

for Iván had just turned sixteen, and Shorty Paco apologized, and from then on it was Señorito Iván here and Señorito Iván there, because, of course, Iván was almost a man, and it was quite reasonable for him to take pride in his hunting prowess, for it was common knowledge that not only did he kill the most birds in one second, he also shot down the highest, swiftest, most distant partridges, nobody else even came close, and without fail he would call on Paco as his witness,

that's a long way off, the Minister said; hey Paco, about how far was I from where I shot that bird on the first beat, the one that fell on the stones after it was way up in the clouds, the one that hit the deck in the Charca de los Galápagos, do you remember?

and wide-eyed, Shorty Paco jutted his chin out proudly,

how could I ever forget? The partridge was flying at least a hundred yards away,

or if the subject was fast partridges, the same refrain,

don't just take my word for it; Paco, you tell them how that partridge flew, the one from the ford that caught me by surprise as I was taking a sip of wine . . . ?

and Paco tilted his head slightly, his finger on his cheek as if deep in thought, yes, heavens,

Señorito Iván persisted,

> the one that was riding that gust of wind, remember,
> near the arbutus, remember what you said, remember
> what you said . . .

and Paco narrowed his eyes as if he were thinking hard, puckered his lips as if about to whistle, although he didn't, and,

> faster than any airplane,

he confirmed, and although Señorito Iván had no idea how far away the other man's farthest partridge was, or how fast it was going when he shot it, his own were invariably the fastest and the farthest away, and to back up his claim, he'd appeal to Shorty Paco, and this buoyed Paco, he was glad that his judgment mattered, and he was happy when he realized that what Señorito Iván's friends most envied were in fact *his* skills and the way *he* retrieved,

> the dog with the keenest scent couldn't do what this man
> does for you, Iván, mark my words, you don't know what
> a treasure you have,

they'd tell him, and Señorito Iván's friends often asked to witness Shorty Paco retrieve a short-winged partridge, and when that happened, they ignored the post-hunt chit-chat and the bickering between the hunting attendants and followed Paco, who'd ask, relishing his role once he was surrounded by the crème de la crème,

> tell me, where did it hit the deck?

and the Secretary, or the Ambassador, or the Minister,

> here are the feathers it dropped, Paco,

and Shorty Paco,

> tell me, in what direction was it going?

and whoever,

> into the brambles, Paco, veering toward the brambles,

and Paco,

tell me, was it alone, in a pair, or in a covey?

and whoever,

there were two, Paco, I think it was a pair,

and Señorito Iván would glance sardonically at his guests and jerk his chin at Shorty Paco, as if to say, what did I tell you? and Shorty Paco would immediately crouch down and sniff the ground hard, two yards from where it hit the deck, and mutter,

it dragged itself this way,

and he'd follow its traces for several yards and, finally, he'd stand up,

it went in this direction, so it must be in that thicket, and

if it's not there, it must have given up the ghost in the

scrub near the cork oak, it can't have gone much further,

and the group would trail after Paco, and just as he'd said, if the bird wasn't in the thicket, it was expiring in the scrub by the cork oak, he was always right, and the awestruck Secretary or Ambassador or Minister, whoever, would say,

and why is it necessarily in one of those two places, Paco?

do tell,

and Shorty Paco would glare at him for a few seconds and then say with ill-concealed contempt,

the partridge keeps a straight line when it's trying to hide,

and they'd look at each other and nod, and Señorito Iván, arms crossed over the chest of his shooting jacket, would smile broadly,

what did I tell you?

as pleased with himself as when he showed off his American rifle or Guita, his griffon puppy, and when he and Paco were once again alone in their shooting blind, he'd comment,

did you see how that French fag can't tell a jay from a
partridge?
or else,
do you realize that fag of an ambassador has got no tact,
that's a serious defect in a diplomat,
because, ineluctably, for Señorito Iván, everyone who grabbed
a hunting gun was a fag except for him, the word was per-
petually on his lips, a real obsession, and occasionally, in the
heat of the hunt, when the voices of the hunters mingled in
the distance and cornets blasted at the far ends, driving the
birds into a narrow space, and the partridges took off, disori-
ented, whrrrr, whrrrr, whrrrr, whrrrr, in every direction, and
the covey quickly entered the sights of the guns and Señorito
Iván downed two here, two there, two with one shot, or two
with a ricochet, and shots rang out left and right, it was like
war, and Shorty Paco silently counted, thirty-three, thirty-
four, thirty-five, and changed the empty gun for a loaded one,
as many as five times, and the barrels were red-hot, he noted
in his head where each bird fell—in those situations Shorty
Paco was on fire like a setter, he couldn't keep still, the urge to
retrieve was stronger than he was, and he'd peer out, crouching down at the end of the blind, muffling his words so as not
to disrupt the hunt,
    let me go, señorito, let me go!
and Señorito Iván, harshly,
    quiet, Paco!
and Shorty Paco, increasingly agitated,
    let me go, señorito, I'm begging you!
and Señorito Iván, still shooting,
    Paco, don't make me lose my cool, wait until this round
    is finished,

but Shorty Paco lost it the second he saw partridges thudding down dead right in front of his nose, he lost it,

let me go, señorito, I'm begging you, for Chrissake!

and he'd beg until Señorito Iván got angry, kicked him in the rear, and said,

if you leave this blind early, Paco, I'll shoot you, you know I will,

but it was only a passing fit of anger, it was all for show, because minutes later, when Shorty Paco began to gather up his booty and appeared with sixty-four of the sixty-five birds that had been shot and told him anxiously,

the partridge that's missing, Señorito Iván, the one you downed on the edge of the broom, Facundo stole it from me, he says it belongs to his señorito,

the señorito's rage now shifted to Facundo,

Facundo!

he thundered, and Facundo ran up,

let's keep this nice and peaceful, that partridge from the broom is mine, so hand it over,

he held out his flattened palm, but Facundo shrugged his shoulders and looked at him blankly,

my señorito downed another bird by the broom, this one's ours,

but Señorito Iván thrust his hand out even further and his fingertips began to itch,

Facundo, don't try me, you know that nothing makes me more furious than people stealing birds that I killed, so give that partridge to me this minute,

and, left with no choice, Facundo handed over the partridge without so much as a word, and as usual, René the Frenchman, a regular at the hunts, until the inevitable happened, was flabbergasted,

how is possible Iván for to kill sixty-five partridges and
Paco to collect sixty-five partridges? Me no understand,
he repeated, and pleased with himself, Shorty Paco smiled slyly and pointed to his head,

I take notes here,
and the Frenchman's eyes grew wide,

aha! you make note in your *tête!*
he exclaimed, and Shorty Paco, back in the blind with Señorito Iván,

he said titty, Señorito Iván, I swear by my mother's grave,
it must mean something different in his language,
and Señorito Iván,

right you are,
and from that day on, whenever they met up without the ladies present, as when they drew lots to determine who would be in which blind, or while they were in the blind during the hunt at midday, Señorito Iván and his guests would say titty instead of head,

this cartridge is so hard, it's giving me a titty-ache,
or else,

the subsecretary is very stubborn, if he gets something
into his titty, he won't let it go,
and they'd rehearse that a hundred times, laughing raucously, chortling until their sides ached, and then the hunt would restart, and once, when the fifth round was finished, at twilight, Señorito Iván fished around in the breast pocket of his shooting jacket and, with great fanfare, handed Paco a hundred-peseta note,

take this, Paco, and don't waste it, because you're costing
me a pretty penny right now and things are a bit tight at
the moment,
and Shorty Paco took the note and stuffed it into his pocket
discreetly,
I won't waste it, señorito, I'll make it last,
and the next morning, Régula and Rogelio took the trailer
to Cordovilla, to the Hashemite's store, to buy cloth or plush
blankets for the boys, so they wouldn't go without, and all
was well except that the last time that Frenchman came,
there was a big argument in the Casa Grande during lunch,
or so Nieves said, on the subject of culture, for Señorito
René said that central Europe was more cultured, a tactless
remark, and Señorito Iván,
that's your opinion, René, but there are no illiterates here
now, or do you think we're still in '36?
and they went back and forth with each other, louder and
louder, until they lost their cool and began trading insults,
and as a last resort, a seething Señorito Iván summoned
Shorty Paco, Régula, and Ceferino,
it's pointless to argue, René, you need to see it with your
own eyes,
he shouted, and when Paco showed up with the others, Señorito Iván adopted Señorito Lucas's didactic tone and told
the Frenchman,
look here, René, frankly, these people were illiterate a
few years ago, but look, Paco, grab the pen and neatly
write your name, please,
and he forced a smile,
because nothing less than the dignity of our nation is at
stake,

and everyone at the whole table was on the edge of their
seats, and Don Pedro the Administrator nervously chewed
the inside of his cheek and put his hand on René's forearm,
    believe it or not, René, for years this country has been
    doing everything humanly possible to redeem these
    people,
and Señorito Iván,
    shhh, don't distract him,
and Shorty Paco, pressured by the pregnant silence, scrib-
bled on the back of the yellow paper that Señorito Iván
had pushed toward him across the table, committing all
five senses to the task, flaring his wide nostrils, and managed a shaky, illegible signature, and when he'd finished, he
straightened up and returned the pen to Señorito Iván, and
Señorito Iván handed it to Ceferino,
    your turn, Ceferino,
he rasped, and a startled Ceferino leaned over the tablecloth
and inscribed his signature, and finally, Señorito Iván addressed Régula,
    now it's your turn, Régula,
and turning to the Frenchman,
    no discrimination here, René, we make no distinction
    between males and females, as you can see,
and Régula had trouble gripping the pen with her flat, stubby
thumb with no fingerprint, yet haltingly, she still managed
to write her name, but Señorito Iván, who was talking to the
Frenchman, didn't notice how painstaking it was, and the
second she finished, he took her right hand and brandished
it repeatedly like a flag,
    what did I tell you?
he said,

tell that to people in Paris, René, because you French-
men are always judging us; if you care to know, until very
recently this woman signed with her thumb, look!

and saying that, he grabbed Régula's deformed thumb, as
flat as a spatula, and Régula was embarrassed and blushed
bright red as if Señorito Iván had stood stark naked on the
table, but René wasn't listening to what Señorito Iván was
saying, he was staring concernedly at Régula's flattened
thumb, and Señorito Iván, noticing how shocked he seemed,
explained,

ah, you know, the thumbs of the women working with
esparto grass are like that, René, it comes with the job,
their fingers are deformed by all the grass braiding, it
can't be helped,

and he laughed and cleared his throat and, to break the tension, looked the three of them in the face and said,

well done, you can go,

and as they shuffled toward the door, Régula muttered,

Señorito Iván does the darndest things,

and around the table, they all laughed indulgently, patron-
izingly, except for René, whose eyes had clouded over and
who sat in a steely, hostile silence, but to tell the truth, things
like this didn't happen often on the Cortijo, life was usually
peaceful enough, punctuated by the señora's periodic visits
that forced Régula to be on the alert so as not to keep her
waiting, for if she ever had to wait even a few minutes for the
car, her chauffeur, Maxi, would soon start grumbling,

where the fuck have you been, we've been stuck here half
an hour,

so nastily that even if they interrupted her in the middle
of changing Tiny, she wouldn't stop to wash her hands, she

would simply come running whenever she heard the horn honk summoning her to slide the bolt out, and the second the Señora Marquesa alighted from the car, she'd wrinkle her nose, for it was almost as sensitive as Shorty Paco's, and say,

> take care when cleaning out those coops, Régula, the odor is most unpleasant,

or something to that effect, but politely, never disrespectfully, and embarrassed, Régula would hide her hands under her apron and,

> yes, señora, we'll do whatever you say,

and the señora would walk slowly through the small garden around every corner of the yard, inspecting every inch, until finally she went up to the Casa Grande and summoned everyone to the room with the big mirror, and one by one, starting with Don Pedro the Administrator and finishing with Ceferino the Pigman, she would ask each and every person about their family and their problems, and when she said goodbye, she'd bestow on them a haughty, thin-lipped smile and hand each of them a shining fifty-peseta coin,

> here you are, so you can celebrate my visit to the Casa Grande in your homes,

each of them except for Don Pedro the Administrator, of course, for Don Pedro the Administrator was like family, and they'd all leave happy as clams,

> the señora is so good to the poor,

they'd each say as they turned the coin over in their palms, and at dusk, they'd bring all the oil lamps into the yard and roast a baby goat and wash it down with wine, and then would come the hurrahs and the high spirits,

> long live Señora Marquesa! may she live for many years!

and, as was the custom, they'd all end up tipsy and merry, and the señora, silhouetted against the lamplit window of her chambers, would raise her arms and wish them good night, and so it went, but on her last visit, the señora, upon emerging from the car with Señorita Miriam, bumped into Azarías by the fountain and, frowning, tossed her head back,

I don't know you, who do you belong to?

she asked, and Régula, cowering, quickly jumped in,

he's my brother, señora,

and the señora,

where is he coming from? he's barefoot,

and Régula,

he was working in La Jara, you see, but at sixty-one they fired him,

and the señora,

well, he's old enough to stop working, so wouldn't he be better off in a charity home somewhere?

and Régula bowed her head, but said forcefully,

while I'm alive, no child of my mother will die in an asylum,

and at that, Señorita Miriam butted in,

mama, what's the harm? there's room for everyone on the Cortijo,

and Azarías stared at the nails of his right hand, then smiled at Señorita Miriam and the empty sky and chewed twice before speaking,

I manure the geraniums every morning,

he said in his slurred voice, justifying himself, and the señora,

that's good of you,

and Azarías, growing more confident by the minute,

and late at night I go to the mountains and give the tawny
owl a good run to keep him away from the Cortijo,
and the señora furrowed her brow, straightened, and leaned
toward Régula,
give the tawny owl a good run? what is he talking about?
and Régula, shrinking back,
it's just one of his things, Azarías isn't a bad fellow, señora, just a bit simple,
but Azarías kept on,
and now I'm looking after kitey,
he smiled, a drop of saliva escaping his mouth, and Señorita
Miriam, once again,
I think he's keeping himself useful, don't you agree,
mama?
and the señora couldn't take her eyes off him, but Azarías,
suddenly, in a friendly gesture, took Señorita Miriam's hand,
bared his gums in a grateful smile, and muttered,
come and see kitey, señorita,
and Señorita Miriam, dragged by the man's herculean
strength, stumbled after him and, turning her head for a
moment, said,
I'm going to see the birdy, mama, don't wait for me, I'll be
up there in no time,
and Azarías led her under the willow, and once there, he
looked up and said, loud but tender,
tchak!
and out of the blue, much to Señorita Miriam's astonishment, a black bird flew gracefully down from the highest
branches and gently settled on Azarías's shoulder, and Azarías took her hand again and,
watch,

he said, and guided her to the stone bench under the window, past the big flowerpot, and he took some bits from the box of meal and offered them to the bird, and the bird swallowed the bits of meal one after another, his appetite seemingly inexhaustible, and Azarías scratched him between the eyes and crooned,

pretty kitey, pretty kitey,

and the bird,

tchak, tchak, tchak!

it asked for more, and Señorita Miriam, fearful,

he's so hungry!

and Azarías kept stuffing meal into its beak and pushing the meal down its throat with his fingertip, and when Azarías was totally engrossed in the bird, Tiny let out a bloodcurdling scream from inside the house, and Señorita Miriam was taken aback,

what is *that?*

she asked, and Azarías, nervously,

it's Tiny,

and he put the box of meal on the bench and then picked it up, put it down, and paced fretfully, the jackdaw on his shoulder, working his jaw up and down, moaning,

I can't be in two places at the same time,

but seconds later, Tiny's piercing shriek sounded again, and Señorita Miriam was terrified,

are you sure that's a little girl?

and Azarías grew increasingly agitated, the little jackdaw eyed them anxiously, and he turned to her, took her by the hand again, and,

come with me,

he said, and they both went into the house together, and Señorita Miriam crept forward tentatively, feeling a sense of foreboding, and when she spotted the girl in the half dark, her little legs thin as strips of wire and her big head slumped on the cushion, tears sprang to her eyes, and she lifted both hands to her mouth,

good God!

she exclaimed, and Azarías looked at her with his gummy smile, but Señorita Miriam couldn't take her eyes off the small crib, she seemed to have turned into a pillar of salt, so stiff, pale, and terrified,

good God,

she repeated, shaking her head quickly from side to side as if trying to banish an evil thought, but Azarías had already taken the child in his arms, and, mumbling inaudibly, he sat on the stool, held the girl's head in the crook of his arm, and, grabbing the jackdaw with his left hand and Tiny's forefinger with his right, he slowly brought her finger close to the animal's brow, and once her finger had stroked it, he suddenly moved her finger away, laughed, and pressed the girl against his body, whispering in that deep, nasal tone of his,

she's a pretty kitey, isn't she, baby?

Book Five
The Accident

When the doves began their passage, Señorito Iván would stay at the Cortijo for several weeks, and every year by that date, Shorty Paco readied the pigeons and tackle and greased the swing for the decoy, so the moment the señorito appeared, they would be off in the Land Rover, down one trail after another, searching for the birds' hideouts, which changed according to the ripening of the acorns, but as the years went by, Shorty Paco found it harder to climb the holm oaks and when Señorito Iván saw him hanging awkwardly on a branch, he'd laugh,

> age forgives nobody, Paco, your backside keeps getting
> heavier and heavier, but that's life for you,

but Shorty Paco, too proud to give up, used a rope to haul himself up the cork oak or holm oak, even though it burned his hands, and he tied the decoy to the most visible part of the tree, on the very top if possible, and from on high, he flared his broad nostrils contentedly at the señorito, as if he could see with them,

> I can still do it, see, señorito?

he cried triumphantly, and firmly astride a sturdy branch, he pulled on the string tied to the decoy so that the cock pigeon lost its balance and fluttered its wings, while Señorito

Iván, concealed in the blind, studied the sky for any movement and told him,

a few dozen stock pigeons, Paco, don't move,

or else,

some wood pigeons, stay quiet, Paco,

or else,

look at those rock pigeons playing, Paco, watch,

and Shorty Paco didn't move, or stayed quiet, or watched the
rock pigeons, but Señorito Iván was rarely happy,

not so jerky, fag, can't you see that when you jerk the
string, it scares them?

and Shorty Paco moved more gently, his hand steadier, until suddenly, half a dozen birds wheeled away from the flock,
and Señorito Iván prepared his gun and sweetened his tone,

careful, they're doubling back,

and at such times, Shorty Paco's tugs became more abrupt
as he tried to ensure that the decoy cock moved but didn't
open his wings completely, and as the birds approached, the
señorito steadied his rifle and took aim and bang-bang!

two! a pair!

Paco exulted among the foliage, and Señorito Iván,

shut your trap,

and bang-bang,

another pair!

Paco cheered from way up high, he couldn't stop himself,
and Señorito Iván,

shut up!

and bang-bang,

that one got away!

lamented Paco, and Señorito Iván,

can't you be quiet for one second, damn fag,

but between one bang-bang and the next, Shorty Paco's legs, hooked around the branch, went numb, and when he slid down the tree, he had to use his hands because his feet wouldn't move, and if he felt anything at all, it was only a bubbly tingling, like soda water, that he couldn't control, but Señorito Iván didn't notice and urged him to find a fresh vantage point, because he liked to change his spot four or five times a day, and by the end of the shoot, Shorty Paco's shoulders hurt, his hands hurt, and his thighs hurt, his whole body felt stiff, and his limbs felt completely numb, but the next morning, off they'd go again, for Señorito Iván couldn't get enough of the cock decoy, he liked that type of shoot as much if not more than hunting partridge, or stalking sandgrouse in the wetlands, or going after woodcocks with Guita the puppy and a hawk bell, yes, Señorito Iván was never satisfied, and in the morning, at daybreak, he was ready to go,

> you tired, Paco?

he smiled maliciously, and added,

> age forgives nobody, Paco, who'd have thought it would come for you, given your talents,

and wanting to prove himself, Shorty Paco climbed the trees more quickly than he had the previous day, he even risked breaking his neck, and he tied the decoy to the crest of the holm oak or cork oak as high as he could, but if the flocks were wary or didn't bite, he shimmied down and relocated to another of their favorite haunts, and so on and so forth, from tree to tree, Shorty Paco expended all his energy, but around Señorito Iván, who had begun to think that Paco was acting strangely, he tried to pretend he was fine, he climbed up again as energetically as ever, but when he was almost at the top, Señorito Iván,

not there, for fuck's sake, Paco, that tree's way too low,
can't you see? find the kind of vantage point you always
used to, don't be so lazy,
and Shorty Paco slid down and looked for another vantage
point in a different tree, and up again, all the way to the top,
he went, holding the decoy, but one morning,

I made a mistake, Señorito Iván, I left the hoods at home,
and Señorito Iván, who had been greedily licking his lips all
morning because the sky was black with hen pigeons above
the holm-oak wood in Las Planas, responded imperiously,

so what? blind the cock and let's not waste any more time,
and Shorty Paco,

should I blind it or make a hood with a handkerchief?
and Señorito Iván,

didn't you hear me?
and without further ado, Shorty Paco steadied himself on the
branch, opened his knife and in a flash gouged out the cock's
eyes, and, suddenly blinded, the bird made a few clumsy,
stunned movements, its jerking disturbed more birds than
usual, and once they were airborne, Señorito Iván shot
nonstop,

Paco, from now on, blind all the cocks, do you hear?
those damn hoods let the light in and the birds don't de-
liver the goods,
and so it went on, day after day, until one afternoon, at the
end of a week and a half of daily trips to the countryside, as
Shorty Paco was climbing down a giant holm oak, his numb
leg buckled, and he fell like a sack and landed two yards from
Señorito Iván, and Señorito Iván, startled, jumped back,

fucking fag, you almost flattened me!

but Paco was writhing on the ground, and Señorito Iván went over and put his hand behind Paco's head,

did you hurt yourself, Paco?

but Shorty Paco couldn't reply, the impact had winded him, and he could only gesture toward his right leg,

oh, that's nothing to worry about . . . !

said Señorito Iván, and he tried to help Shorty Paco to his feet, but Shorty Paco leaned against the trunk of the holm oak and said, when at last he could speak,

this leg won't support me, Señorito Iván, it's gone to sleep,

and Señorito Iván,

it won't support you, come on now, don't be squeamish, Paco, if you don't move it, it will only get worse,

but Shorty Paco tried to take a step and fell down,

I can't, señorito, it's no use, I felt the bone crack,

and Señorito Iván,

for fuck's sake, don't cop out, fag, who's going to fix the decoy for all the wood pigeons over in Las Planas?

and Shorty Paco, on the ground, feeling truly guilty, his face contorted in pain, tried to placate him,

perhaps Quirce, my boy, he can follow instructions, Señorito Iván, he's a bit sullen, but he can help you out,

and Señorito Iván took a few steps, then looked down, he hesitated, but finally he went to the end of the copse, cupped his hands, and shouted toward the Cortijo, once, twice, three times, more loudly, more impatiently, more viciously each time, and, when nobody responded to his hollering, he became livid and began to swear, and finally he turned to Shorty Paco,

are you absolutely sure you can't stand up, Paco?

and Shorty Paco, slumped against the trunk of the holm oak,
    there's no way, Señorito Iván,
and, all of a sudden, in the distance, Facundo's older boy
peered out of the gate into the yard, and Señorito Iván took
a white handkerchief out of his pocket and waved repeatedly, and Facundo's boy waved his arms like the sails of a
windmill, and a quarter of an hour later he was by their side
gasping for air, for when Señorito Iván called, you didn't
wait, everybody knew that, especially when he was carrying
a gun, and Señorito Iván placed his hands on his shoulders
and gripped him hard so he'd realize how important his task
was, and told him,
    get two people to come, you hear? get someone to help
    Paco, who's hurt himself, and get Quirce to help me out,
    got it?
and as he spoke, the tan, bright-eyed boy nodded, and Señorito Iván jerked his chin at Shorty Paco and said, by way of
explanation,
    that fag had a bad fall, couldn't have happened at a worse
    time,
and before long, two came from the Cortijo and took Paco
away on a stretcher, and Señorito Iván went into the copse
with Quirce, trying to establish some kind of bond, but
Quirce was sulky, yes-maybe-no gruff, surly, unresponsive,
as though he were dumb, but on the other hand, he was ex-
cellent with the decoy, a real natural, smart, you only had
to say hard, gentle, quiet, fast, he followed orders to the letter, and his movements were so rapid the wood pigeons doubled back unsuspectingly right over the decoy, and Señorito
Iván, bang-bang! bang-bang! firing nonstop, not keeping

up, missing time and again, and each time he missed, he swore like a sailor, but most frustrating of all, frankly, was that he couldn't blame anyone but himself, and to make matters worse, he was mortified that Quirce was witness to his misses, and he told him,

your father's fall must have made me shaky, boy, I never miss like this,

and Quirce, hidden in the leaves, replied casually,

maybe,

and Señorito Iván lost it,

there's no maybe about it, for fuck's sake, it's God's honest truth, it's gospel,

bang-bang! bang-bang! bang-bang!

another fag got away!

Señorito Iván screamed, and Quirce, up above, was dead silent, motionless, as if he weren't there, and as soon as they were back at the farmstead, Señorito Iván dropped by Paco's house,

how are we, Paco, how're you feeling?

and Shorty Paco,

okay, Señorito Iván,

his leg was stretched over a stool and his ankle had swollen up like a tire,

it's a bad break, did you hear the bone snap?

but Señorito Iván was only interested in his own needs,

I've never missed as many pigeons as I did this morning, Paco, can you believe it? I was like a beginner, I can't imagine what your son must think of me!

and Shorty Paco,

it was just nerves, it's normal,

and Señorito Iván,

   normal, what do you mean normal? don't make excuses,
   do you really think it's normal, Paco, with all the hours of
   hunting I've clocked, for me to miss a cross-eyed stock pigeon, from here to the geraniums? come on, Paco, have
   you ever seen me miss a cross-eyed pigeon from here to
   the geraniums?

and Quirce behind him, holding the pole of pigeons in one
hand and cradling the gun in the other, was taciturn and silent, and suddenly Azarías appeared in the doorway, under
the vine, barefoot, his feet filthy, pants around his knees,
moaning like a puppy, offering his gummy smile, and Shorty
Paco, slightly taken aback, gestured to him,

   my brother-in-law,

he said, and Señorito Iván looked Azarías up and down,

   well, you've sure got a handsome family,

he commented, but Azarías, as if attracted by some magnetic
force, slowly walked toward the pole, looked longingly at the
dead pigeons, and suddenly touched and stroked them one
by one with his fingers, felt their claws and beaks, checking
whether they were young or old, male or female, and, after a
while, he turned his watery gaze to Señorito Iván,

   shall I pluck them for you?

he asked hopefully, and Señorito Iván,

   do you know how?

and Shorty Paco chimed in,

   of course, it's the only thing he ever does,

and with that, Señorito Iván took the pole of pigeons from
Quirce and handed it over to Azarías,

   here you are,

he said,

and when you've plucked them, take them to Doña Purita, on my behalf, will you remember? and as for you,
Paco, look alive, we're off to Cordovilla to see the doctor,
I don't like the look of that leg, and we have a hunt on the
twenty-second,

and between Señorito Iván, Quirce, and Régula, they settled
Shorty Paco in the Land Rover, and once in Cordovilla, Don
Manuel the Doctor felt his ankle, tried to move it, X-rayed it
twice, and, when he'd finished, raised his eyebrows,

I don't even need to see the X-rays, it's his fibula,

he said, and Señorito Iván,

his what?

it's fractured,

but Señorito Iván refused to heed the doctor's words,

you're joking, Manolo, on the twenty-second we have a
hunt on the estate, I can't do without him,

and Don Manuel, with his piercing black eyes like an inquis-
itor's, his neck straight, as if it had been smoothed with a
trowel,

I'm telling you what I know, Iván, you do what you want,
you're the donkey's master,

and Señorito Iván snarled, put out,

it's not like that, Manolo,

and the doctor,

all I can do for now is give him a splint, the injury is very
tender, and a plaster cast wouldn't help at the moment,
bring him back in a week,

and Shorty Paco was silent and looked sheepishly from one
to the other,

these ankle fractures aren't serious, but they're trouble,
I'm sorry, Iván, but you'll have to find yourself another
hunting attendant,
and Señorito Iván looked perplexed for a few seconds, and
then,
this is a fucking mess, and it's only by a stroke of luck that
he fell right there,
he said, pointing to the edge of the carpet,
it's a miracle the fag didn't break my neck,
and after conversing for a few minutes, the señorito and
Shorty Paco went back to the Cortijo, and after a week had
gone by, Señorito Iván went to pick up Shorty Paco in the Land
Rover, and they drove back to Cordovilla, but before the doctor could remove the splint, Señorito Iván was all over him,
Manolo, can't you fix it so he'll be all right on the twenty-
second?
but the doctor turned his flat, smooth neck vigorously,
but if the twenty-second were, say, the day after tomorrow, Iván, this man needs forty-five days in a plaster cast,
though sure, you could buy him a couple of crutches so
he can start moving around at home in a week or so,
and once he'd finished putting the plaster on, Shorty Paco
and Señorito Iván started the drive back to the Cortijo and
traveled in silence, feeling a gulf growing between them
as if something had ruptured, and now and then Shorty
Paco sighed, feeling responsible, and he tried to relieve the
tension,
please believe me, I am really sorry, Señorito Iván,
but Señorito Iván, staring through the windshield with a
scowl on his face as he drove, said nothing, and Shorty Paco
smiled and made an effort to move his leg,

this old fellow weighs a ton,

he began, but Señorito Iván, pensive as he dodged the potholes, didn't flinch until Shorty Paco tried again for the third time, when he burst out,

look, Paco, the doctors can say what they want, but you can't sit back, you have to try to walk; my grandmother, may she rest in peace, did nothing, and, as you know, she was crippled for the rest of her days; in these cases, with or without crutches, you need to move, go out into the fields even if it hurts; if you do nothing, you're done for, I'm telling you,

and when they drove through the gate to the Cortijo, they came across Azarías in the yard, with the jackdaw on his shoulder, and when he heard the engine, he turned toward them and walked over to the Land Rover's passenger-seat window and laughed, saliva dripping from his mouth,

you didn't want to go after the kiteys, did you, Quirce?

he asked, stroking the jackdaw, but Quirce just peered at Señorito Iván with his sullen eyes, dark and round like a woodcock's, and Señorito Iván jumped out of the vehicle, fascinated by the black bird perching on Azarías's shoulder,

so you can tame birds too?

he asked, and put out his hand to grab the bird, but it spooked and gave a great *tchak* and flew off to the chapel eaves, and Azarías laughed, working his jaw from side to side,

she gets scared,

he said, and Señorito Iván,

that's only natural, I'm not surprised, it doesn't know me,

and he looked up toward the bird,

will it come down from there?

he asked, and Azarías,

will she come down? just you wait,
and he produced a velvety, full-throated *tchak,* and the jackdaw hovered back and forth anxiously for a few seconds, tilted
its head to glance at the yard, and finally dove into space;
wings open wide, gliding, it circled the vehicle twice before
landing on Azarías's shoulder and pecking the gray hair on
his neck as if looking for lice, and Señorito Iván, amazed,

that's funny, it can fly, but it doesn't fly away,
and Shorty Paco went over to them, gingerly resting the weight
of his body on his crutches, and addressed Señorito Iván,

he raised it and trained it, you see,
and Señorito Iván, increasingly intrigued,

and what does this animal do during the day?
and Shorty Paco,

a little bit of everything, it picks bark off cork oaks, it looks
for glass, it sharpens its beak on the stone edge of the
trough, sometimes it takes a nap in the willow branches,

it really does whatever it wants,
and while Paco talked, Señorito Iván looked Azarías up and
down, and after a while, he glanced at Shorty Paco and whispered over his shoulder as if talking to himself,

I say, Paco, with all those skills he has, wouldn't your
brother-in-law make a good hunting attendant?
but Shorty Paco shook his head, shifted his weight to his
left foot in order to point his right finger toward his head,
and said,

maybe with the decoy pigeon, but he's too simpleminded
to handle partridges,
and from that day on, Señorito Iván visited Shorty Paco every morning and urged him on,

Paco, move, for fuck's sake, don't stay still, you look like
an invalid, don't forget what I told you,
but Shorty Paco looked at him with the melancholy eyes of
a sick retriever,
that's easy for you to say, Señorito Iván,
and Señorito Iván,
look, it's almost the twenty-second,
and Shorty Paco,
what can we do? I'm really sorry, Señorito Iván,
and Señorito Iván,
"I'm really sorry, I'm really sorry," you fucking liar, the
measure of a man is his strength of will, Paco, for fuck's
sake, where there's no will, there's no man. Paco, think
straight, you have to try even though it hurts; if not, you'll
never be able to live your life, you'll be useless for the
rest of your days, do you understand?
and Señorito Iván harassed and taunted him, until Shorty
Paco sobbed and spluttered,
when I put my foot down, it feels like someone's slicing
through the sole of my foot with a handsaw, it's really
painful,
and Señorito Iván,
that's just fear and anxiety, Paco, don't the crutches make
a difference?
and Shorty Paco,
a little, but only if I move slowly and only on flat ground,
but dawn broke on the 22nd, and Señorito Iván, come what
may, drove up to Shorty Paco's door at first light in his brown
Land Rover,
come on, get up, Paco, we'll be careful, don't worry,

and Shorty Paco walked over to him hesitantly, and as soon as he smelled the polish on his boots and the thyme and lavender on Señorito Iván's pants, he forgot all about his leg and climbed into the vehicle while Régula fretted,

I sincerely hope we won't regret this, Señorito Iván, and Señorito Iván,

don't worry, Régula, I'll bring him back in one piece, and in the Casa Grande the señoritos from Madrid were delighted with the preparations, the Minister, and the Count, and Señorita Miriam, who also liked to shoot on the occasional hunt, they were all smoking and chattering loudly while they feasted on coffee and fried breadcrumb hash, and when Paco came into the dining room, their excitement only grew, for Shorty Paco seemed to energize their interest in the hunt, and everyone responded differently,

so wonderful to see you, Paco!

how did you manage to fall, Paco, for fuck's sake? at least you didn't smash your face in,

and as the Ambassador quietly tried to explain Shorty Paco's hunting talents, Paco tried to respond to one group and then another, and emphasized his words by pushing his crutches forward as proof,

pardon me for not taking my cap off, and they,

no need for that, Paco,

and Señorita Miriam, with that open, luminous smile of hers,

will we have a good day, Paco?

and the guests fell silent before his imminent prediction, and Shorty Paco shared his verdict,

it's a clear morning, and if things don't take a turn for the worse, I bet we'll be in business, and at that, Señorito Iván removed from the Florentine chest the leather case, blackened by so much handling over time, the one containing the mother-of-pearl tokens, and someone declared,

it's the moment of truth,

and one by one, ceremonially, as if practicing an ancient ritual, they each drew a token with a number on it,

we'll go in pairs,

Señorito Iván advised, and the Count was the first to consult his token, and he exclaimed heartily,

nine!

and without explaining himself, he stupidly began to clap, and he applauded so enthusiastically, his face radiated so much joy, that the Minister walked over to him,

is nine a good number, Count?

and the Count,

> a good number, are you kidding? it's stony ground, under a crag, by the ford, where they hurtle down like fools, and by the time they spot you, it's too late for them to retreat; I collared forty-three last year from that blind,

and, meanwhile, Señorito Iván jotted down the names of the guns next to the corresponding numbers, and once he'd finished, he tucked his notebook into the top pocket of his shooting jacket,

let's get a move on, it's late,

he urged them, and they each climbed into their respective Land Rovers with their respective hunting attendants, their sets of twin guns and cartridge pouches, while Crespo the Gamekeeper packed the beaters, bugles, and markers into the tractor trailers, and finally they all set off, and Señorito Iván made all kinds of accommodations for Shorty Paco, which was quite unusual for him, placing Paco near the decoy in the Jeep and, as they headed into cross-country terrain, going off the trails and even, when necessary, carefully fording shallow streams,

> Paco, wait here, don't move, I'm going to hide the vehicle behind those holm oaks,

in other words, it seemed that everything was fine apart from the retrieving, for Paco moved slowly and nervously on his crutches, and the hunting attendants from nearby blinds took advantage of his lack of speed and snagged his dead birds,

> Señorito Iván, Ceferino took two partridges that weren't his,

he complained, and Señorito Iván, in a rage,

> Ceferino, bring me those two birds, you motherfucker, I swear you're not going to use Paco's injury to take advantage of him while he's down,

he cried, but on other occasions, it was Facundo, or Ezequiel the Pigman, and Señorito Iván couldn't keep track of them all, it was impossible to fight on all fronts, and his mood darkened, his tone became harsh,

> for fuck's sake, can't you move any quicker, Paco, you're like a steamroller, if you don't watch out, they'll steal the pants out from under you,

and Shorty Paco tried hard, but the uneven ground made it hard for him to find his footing, and when he tried to move faster, bang! he hit the ground like a sack of potatoes,

> ay, Señorito Iván, the bone cracked again, I felt it!

and Señorito Iván, who, for the first time in the history of the Cortijo had five fewer birds than the Count by the third round, was beside himself and upbraided Paco,

> for fuck's sake, Paco, what's wrong with you now? you've been acting like a fag for far too long, don't you think?

but Shorty Paco insisted from the ground,

señorito, I've broken the bone again,

and Señorito Iván's curses could be heard as far away as Cordovilla,

can't you move? at least try to stand up, man,

but Shorty Paco couldn't even try, he simply collapsed into a furrow and cradled his fractured leg in his hands, ignoring Señorito Iván's curses, and finally Señorito Iván relented,

all right, Paco, Crespo will take you home now, you go to bed, and this afternoon, when we finish, I'll take you to see Don Manuel,

and, hours later, Don Manuel the doctor remarked abruptly when he saw him,

you should have been more careful,

and Shorty Paco tried to justify himself,

I—

but Señorito Iván was in a hurry and butted in,

get moving, Manolo, I left the Minister all alone,

and the doctor, angrily,

well, naturally he fractured it again, it's a greenstick fracture, absolute immobility,

and Señorito Iván,

what about tomorrow? what the hell am I going to do tomorrow, Manolo? I'm not messing around, I'm telling you,

and the doctor, taking off his white coat,

do whatever you want, Iván, if you want to do this man in for the rest of his days, that's your call,

and back in the brown Land Rover, in a cold fury, Señorito Iván lit one cigarette after another, not looking at Shorty Paco, as if he'd done it on purpose,

another one of your fag tricks,

he hissed repeatedly, and Shorty Paco said nothing, he felt the dampness of the new plaster on his calf, and when they crossed the Tapas ford, the mastiffs howled and ran after the Jeep, and their barking seemed to stir Señorito Iván out of his mood, and he shook his head as if he wanted to chase away a ghost and asked Shorty Paco all of a sudden,

which of your two boys is smarter?

and Paco,

they're both quick learners,

and Señorito Iván,

and what's the name of the one who handled the decoy the other day?

Quirce, Señorito Iván, he's more handy,

and Señorito Iván, after a pause,

he's not very chatty,

and Paco,

no, he's not, señor, it's just how he is, the youth these days,

and Señorito Iván, lighting another cigarette,

Paco, can you tell me what's gotten into the youth? they're never content,

and the next morning with the decoy, Señorito Iván felt challenged by Quirce's persistent ill humor, his total indifference,

are you bored?

he asked him, and Quirce,

yes, no, what does it matter,

and he shut up again, as if not even part of the hunt, but he loaded the twin guns quickly and confidently and swiftly located the downed partridges without a single error, but when it was tipping time, he became haughty when he saw how greedy the other hunting attendants were, and Señorito Iván roared,

Ceferino, you fag, don't try to pull one over on the new kid, come on, give him his due!

and, brought together by the decoy, in an almost familiar manner, Señorito Iván tried to cajole Quirce, to spark even the slightest interest, but the boy, with nothing more than a yes, no, maybe, possibly, was ever more distant and impervious, and Señorito Iván, charging up like an electric battery as soon as the hunt was over, launched into speech in the Casa Grande's vast dining room,

I'm telling you, Minister, young people don't know what they want, this blessed season of peace has been far too easy for them, I reckon they need some war, I'm telling you, people have never had it so good, everybody's got pesetas in their pockets, that's my opinion, never being short of cash makes them arrogant; do you know what Paco's son did to me this afternoon?

and the Minister looked at him out of the corner of his eye as he devoured his filet mignon, and carefully wiped his white napkin across his lips,

I'm all ears,

and Señorito Iván,

it's simple, at the end of the shoot, I handed him a hundred-peseta note, twenty duros, right? and what does he say? forget it, don't bother, and I say, go have a few drinks on me, man, and he goes, I already said thanks but no thanks; only a few days ago, his father, Paco—thank you so much, Señorito Iván, or I can't thank you enough, Señorito Iván—showed proper respect, but I guess the youth of today don't like the idea of hierarchy, though that's just my opinion, Minister, maybe I'm wrong, but we have to know our place, there are the haves and the

have-nots, there's an upper class and a lower class, and
that's life, right?

and his rant hung in the air for a few seconds while the Minister nodded and chewed, unable to reply, and once he'd finished swallowing his mouthful, he graciously wiped his lips
on his white napkin and declared,

a crisis of authority is affecting every level of society
today,

and everyone around the table seemed to agree, with nods
and sounds of assent, and meanwhile Nieves changed their
plates, removing dirty plates with her left hand and replacing them with her right, silent and meek, and Señorito Iván
studied the girl's movements, and when Nieves reached
him, he suddenly looked her square in the face, and the girl
blushed scarlet, and then he said,

tell me, girl, why is your brother Quirce so sullen?

and Nieves gulped and shrugged her shoulders and smiled
faintly and finally put a clean plate on the table to his right
with a shaking hand, and she carried on like that during the
whole dinner, getting everything wrong, and at night, when
it was time to go to bed, Señorito Iván summoned her back,

girl, pull this boot off my foot, it won't budge and I can't
get it off,

and the girl tugged on the boot, first the toe, then the heel,
toe-heel, toe-heel, bobbing it up and down until the boot
came off, and then Señorito Iván lazily raised his other leg,

the other one now, girl, finish the job,

and when Nieves removed the other boot, Señorito Iván
rested his bare feet on the carpet and stared at the girl, smiling imperceptibly,

did you know that you have a very nice figure?

and the embarrassed Nieves whispered,

    if the señorito doesn't need anything else . . .

but Señorito Iván burst out laughing, a loud, exultant laugh,

    I say, girl, none of you behave as well as your father,

    Paco, don't you like it when I compliment you?

and Nieves,

    that's not it, Señorito Iván,

and Señorito Iván took his cigarette case from his pocket, tapped the cigarette on her, and lit it,

    how old are you, girl?

and Nieves,

    I'll be fifteen soon, Señorito Iván,

and Señorito Iván leaned back in his armchair and blew smoke in gently spiraling wisps, enjoying himself,

    you're still very young, you may go,

he allowed, but when Nieves reached the door, he shouted,

    but tell that brother of yours not to be so sour next time,

and Nieves left, but in the kitchen, she couldn't stop washing the dishes, even though she chipped plates and smashed a tureen, so Leticia from Cordovilla, who came up to the Cortijo when there was a hunt, asked her,

    what's gotten into you tonight, girl?

but Nieves stayed silent, she couldn't shake her nerves, and when she finished her duties after midnight, as she crossed the garden on her way home, she spotted Señorito Iván and Doña Purita under the pergola in the pavilion, locked in a passionate, moonlit embrace.

Book Six
The Crime

A hesitant, fearful Don Pedro the Administrator showed up at Shorty Paco's house, acting pompous as usual, although the corner of his mouth kept twitching toward his right ear, betraying his anxiety,

so you didn't see the señora leave, Doña Purita, I mean, Régula?

and Régula,

no, Don Pedro, she didn't leave through the front gate, I'm telling you, we only unbolted it once last night to let Señorito Iván's car out,

and Don Pedro the Administrator,

are you absolutely sure of that, Régula?

and Régula,

Don Pedro, I saw it with my own eyes,

and at her side, Shorty Paco, leaning on his crutches, confirmed what Régula said, and Azarías just smiled, jackdaw on his shoulder, and since he couldn't get any clarity on the situation, Don Pedro the Administrator gave up, left them, and walked off through the yard toward the Casa Grande, head down, shoulders hunched, patting the pockets of his overcoat as if he'd lost his wallet rather than his wife, and when he was out of sight, Nieves came to the doorstep holding Charito in her arms and blurted out,

father, Doña Purita was all over Señorito Iván in the pavilion last night, you should have seen them kissing!

she looked down almost apologetically, and Shorty Paco
moved forward on his crutches until he was face to face with
Nieves,

you keep your mouth shut, girl,

alarmed,

does anyone know you saw them together?

and Nieves,

who could have? it was past midnight and there wasn't a
soul in the Casa Grande,

and Shorty Paco, whose eyes and sensitive broad nostrils
were trembling anxiously, spoke even more softly,

not a word of this to anyone, you hear me? in these matters concerning the señoritos, if you see or hear something, you don't say a word,

but they hadn't even finished the conversation before Don
Pedro the Administrator came back looking frantic, his
heavy jacket unbuttoned and his tie missing, his large hairy
hands dangling down by his sides, and his jaw sagging as if
out of joint,

Doña Purita is definitely not in the house,

he said, and, after a brief pause,

Doña Purita is nowhere to be found, alert all the em-
ployees on the Cortijo, Doña Purita could have been kid-
napped, and here we are, arms crossed, wasting time,

but *his* arms weren't crossed, he was wringing his hands
and eyeing father and daughter, distraught, and Shorty Paco
went house by house, alerting the farmhands, and once
they were all gathered together, Don Pedro the Administrator climbed onto the water trough and announced that Doña
Purita had disappeared,

after I went to bed, she stayed in the Casa Grande to su-
pervise the cleanup, but I haven't seen her since, did any
of you see Doña Purita after midnight last night?
and the men exchanged glances, each keeping a straight
face, and the odd one eased his bottom lip up over his top
lip to signal total ignorance, they all shook their heads, and
Shorty Paco stared at Nieves, but Nieves didn't flinch and
kept rocking Charito from side to side, saying nothing, a
blank look on her face, then suddenly Don Pedro the Administrator squared up to her, and Nieves, startled, blushed
a bright red,

girl,

he said,

you were in the Casa Grande when we left, and Doña Purita was still cleaning up, did you see her after that?
and Nieves, nonplussed, shook her head to the rhythm of
her rocking, and after her denial, Don Pedro the Administrator kept patting the thick pockets of his heavy jacket,
and the right corner of his mouth twitched as he chewed his
cheek,

very well,

he said,

you can go,

he turned to Régula,

Régula, wait a minute,

and when he was face to face with Régula, he dropped all
his defenses,

Doña Purita must have left with him, I mean, with
Señorito Iván, Régula, to make a fool of me, that's the
only reason she would do it, she must have left through
the front gate, there can be no other explanation,
and Régula,

look, I'm positive she wasn't with Señorito Iván, Don Pedro, Señorito Iván was by himself, I swear, and all he said to me was look after that man of yours, Paco, because I'll be needing the decoy before the end of the month and I'll need him, that's all he said to me, and I unbolted the gate and he drove off,

but Don Pedro the Administrator was losing patience,

Señorito Iván was driving the Mercedes, right, Régula?

and Régula arched her brow,

look, Don Pedro, you know I don't know a lot about that kind of thing, the Mercedes is the blue car, right?

Don Pedro nodded, and contorted his face in one strange grimace after another, and Régula thought his face would never look normal again,

one more thing, Régula, did you notice . . . did you notice by any chance if he was carrying a raincoat, clothes, or a suitcase in the back seat?

and Régula,

to tell you the truth, no, I didn't, Don Pedro,

and Don Pedro tried to smile, tried to act casual, but his smile transformed into an icy snarl, and his lips clenched as if he were feeling terribly nauseous, and he whispered into Régula's ear,

Régula, think twice before you give me an answer, couldn't . . . couldn't Doña Purita have been in the car, lying in the back seat perhaps, covered by a coat or some other garment? it's not that I'm suspicious, but she could have been playing a joke on me and gone off to Madrid to make me jealous,

and Régula, her gaze narrowing by the second, remained in denial, listen, I only saw Señorito Iván, and when I went over, he told me, Régula, look after that man for me, Paco, okay?

Don Pedro interrupted angrily,

sure, sure, sure . . .

you already said that, Régula,

and he spun around and strode off, and from that point on he began to wander aimlessly around the Cortijo, head hung low, shoulders hunched, as if trying to make himself as small as possible, now and then slapping his hands inside his long jacket's big pockets against his thighs, all out of sorts, and a week went by like that, and the following Saturday when the Mercedes honked outside the gate, Don Pedro started trembling and clasped his hands so nobody would notice and rushed to the gate, and while Régula removed the bolt, he tried to calm down, and once the car entered the compound and glided gently between the beds of geraniums, everybody could see that Señorito Iván was alone, wearing his zippered leather jacket, his neck wrapped in a scarf, a thin corduroy cap shading his right eye, and, below that, a broad white smile gleaming against his golden tan, and Don Pedro the Administrator couldn't hide his anxiety and right there in the yard, in front of Régula and Shorty Paco, both of whom were standing on the doorstep, he asked,

hey, Iván, you didn't by any chance see Purita the other night after the meal? I have no idea what happened to her, she's nowhere to be found on the Cortijo . . .

and as he spoke, Señorito Iván's smile grew wider and his teeth glimmered, he rakishly flicked his cap so that it lifted up slightly and revealed his forehead and the line of his jet-black hair, and,

don't tell me you've lost your wife, Pedro, what a riot, you
probably had a quarrel and now she's at her mother's
awaiting your arrival?
and Don Pedro shrugged his bony shoulders up and down,
because in one week this man had aged twenty years, and,
Holy Mother of God, his cheeks were so gaunt and so pale
they looked blue, and his mouth twisted and turned until finally he confessed,

    a quarrel, yes, we bickered, Iván, things being what they
are, but tell me, how did she get out of the Cortijo, since
Régula has sworn time and again that she removed the
bolt only for you, I mean, you know that if she'd tried to
sneak off through the holm oaks, the mastiffs would have
torn her apart, you know what those dogs are like, Iván,
they're worse than any wild beast,

and Señorito Iván twirled a lock of black hair with his right
forefinger, seemingly deep in thought, and after a while
he said,

    if you quarreled, maybe she hid in my trunk or in the
space behind the back seat, the Mercedes is quite roomy,
I mean, she could have slipped in without my noticing
and then gotten out in Cordovilla or Fresno when I filled
up on gas, or maybe even in Madrid? my mind was on
other things, I wouldn't have noticed . . .

and Don Pedro the Administrator's eyes shining with tears,
    of course, Iván, that very well may be,
he said, and Señorito Iván straightened the top of his cap,
smiled broadly and generously once more, and patted Don
Pedro the Administrator affectionately on the shoulder
through the car window,

don't let your imagination run away with you, Pedro,
I know you like a bit of drama, Purita loves you, you
know that,
he laughed,
you've got nothing to worry about, you can sleep peacefully,
and he laughed again and, leaning forward, started the engine and drove to the Casa Grande, but before dinner, he was
back at Shorty Paco's,
how's that leg, Paco? I forgot to ask you before Don Pedro
got into such a tizzy,
and Shorty Paco,
okay, Señorito Iván, slowly but surely,
and Señorito Iván crouched down until they were face to
face and declared,
Paco, I bet you don't have the balls to take the decoy out
tomorrow,
and Shorty Paco stared at Señorito Iván in amazement, trying to guess whether he was being serious or was joking, but
as he couldn't decide, he asked,
are you being serious or are you joking, Señorito Iván?
and Señorito Iván crossed his thumb over his index finger,
kissed it, and looked somber,
I'm serious, Paco, I swear, I never joke about hunting,
and I have to be frank with you and say I don't like going with your boy Quirce, he acts as if he were doing me
a favor, and that's not right, Paco, you know if I don't feel
comfortable out in the field, I'd just as soon stay home,
but Shorty Paco pointed at his plaster cast,
but Señorito Iván, how can I possibly go with this?
and Señorito Iván lowered his eyes,

fair enough,

he concurred, but after hesitating for a few seconds, he suddenly looked up,

> and what about your brother-in-law, the moron with the
> jackdaw? you said one time that he could handle the de-
> coy pigeon,

and Shorty Paco tilted his head to one side,

> Azarías is simple, but I guess you can try, there's no harm
> in trying,

and he turned toward the row of mill cottages, a vine growing above each of the front doors, and hollered,

> Azarías!

and after a while, Azarías came out, pants around his knees,
smiling his wet smile, working his jaw up and down,

> Azarías,

said Shorty Paco,

> Señorito Iván wants to take you to the fields tomorrow
> with the decoy—

> with my kitey?

responded Azarías in wonderment,

> no, Azarías, it's not a kitey, it's the decoy, the blind pi-
> geons, you know what I mean? you have to tie them to
> the top of a holm oak, make them move by pulling the
> string, and wait . . .

Azarías nodded,

> like you did in La Jara?

he asked,

> just like in La Jara, Azarías,

replied Shorty Paco, and the following morning, at seven
o'clock sharp, Señorito Iván was waiting by his door in the
brown Land Rover,

Azarías!

señorito!

they moved silently like shadows in the predawn darkness, and the only sound was the smack of Azarías's mouth as he worked his jaw up and down, and when dawn broke over the distant line of mountains,

> put the tools and the pigeon cage in the back, do you have the climbing rope? you're going to climb the trees barefoot? won't your feet get scratched?

but Azarías wasn't listening, he was already preparing the gear, but before they set off, without asking Señorito Iván's permission, he went over to the shed, got the box of meal, went into the yard and looked up, half opened his lips and,

> tchak!

he called in a velvety, nasal tone, and from the top of the weather vane the jackdaw replied to his call,

> tchak!

and the bird looked down toward the shadows moving around the car, and although it wasn't yet light in the yard, it leaned forward and launched itself into space, circling the group before finally landing on Azarías's shoulder, half opening its wings to keep its balance, and then it jumped onto his forearm and opened its beak, and Azarías fed it bits of meal while he drooled and whispered,

> pretty kitey, pretty kitey,

and Señorito Iván,

> it's amazing, that bird eats more meal than it's worth, can't it feed itself yet?

and Azarías's face broke into a gummy smile,

> what can we do if she doesn't know how!

and once it was full, as Señorito Iván was approaching, the jackdaw flew off, and when it was near the chapel door, it soared gracefully, circled back, and settled in the eaves, looking down at them, and Azarías smiled up at it and waved goodbye, and from inside the Jeep, he waved again through the back window as Señorito Iván turned the car onto the mountain trail, and they made their way up to the clump of holm oaks at El Moro, and after they alighted from the car, Azarías peed on his hands under a tree, and when he'd finished, he vigorously climbed the fattest holm oak, hooking his hands around the thickest branch and swinging his flexed legs through the gap in his arms like a monkey, and Señorito Iván,

why do you need that thick rope, Azarías?
and Azarías,

why do I need it, señorito? pass it to me,
and Señorito Iván lifted up the decoy with the blinded pigeon tied to it,

how old are you, Azarías?
and from the top Azarías held the decoy in his left hand,

a year older than señorito,
he replied, and Señorito Iván, perplexed,

which señorito you talking about, Azarías?
and Azarías, while he secured the swing with the decoy attached,

the señorito,
and Señorito Iván,

the one in La Jara?
and Azarías, seated on the thick branch, didn't reply, he simply leaned back on the trunk and smiled contentedly at the vast sky while Señorito Iván gathered some dry branches to

camouflage the hunting blind under the holm oak, and once he'd finished, he peered at the horizon to the south, pale blue in the early morning mist, and frowned,

not a sign of life, we're not too late in the season, I hope? but Azarías was playing with the swing, one-two, one-two, one-two, as if it were a toy, and the blinded pigeon tied to the bar frantically fluttered its wings so as not to fall off, and Azarías smiled a pink gummy smile, and Señorito Iván,

stop it, Azarías, don't drive the bird crazy, it doesn't make

sense to swing it when there are no birds around,
but Azarías kept tugging on the swing, one-two, one-two, one-two, like a child, and Señorito Iván, who hadn't spotted a single pigeon in the sky and was anticipating a failed morning expedition, became angrier by the minute,

for fuck's sake, Azarías, I said, stop it, didn't you hear me? and his threatening tone frightened Azarías, so smiling toothlessly at the angels like a baby on the breast, he went quiet, his rear firmly planted on the branch, until after a while, five stock pigeons flew up, five black dots in the pale blue firmament, and in the blind Señorito Iván steadied his gun and whispered out of the side of his mouth,

they're coming, Azarías, tug now,
and Azarías grabbed the end of the string and tugged,

that's right, go,
but the pigeons ignored the decoy, wheeled to the right, and disappeared over the horizon in the same direction they came from, then a quarter of an hour later, a bigger flock appeared from the southeast, but the same scenario: the birds spurned the blinded male decoy and turned back over the holm oaks in Alcornoque, much to Señorito Iván's rage and despair,

they're not interested, the fucking bitches! get down,
Azarías, let's go to Alisón, it looks as if a few of them are
rallying there,

and Azarías clambered down with the swing on his back,
and they jumped into the Land Rover and dodged the boulders on the way to Alisón, and once they were on the hill,
Azarías peed on his hands, climbed nimbly up a giant cork
oak, attached the decoy, and waited, but there didn't seem to
be any movement there either, although it was too early to
draw that conclusion, but in no time Señorito Iván had lost
all patience,

come down, Azarías, this place is like a cemetery, I don't
like it one bit, this is starting to look hopeless,

and they changed position again, but the hen pigeons, so
few and far between, were suspicious, they weren't fooled,
and already by midmorning Señorito Iván was bored by so
much waiting around, and like a lunatic, he started shooting
left and right, at thrushes and starlings, at blue crows and
magpies, and between shots, he screamed like a madman,

these fuckers say no, no means no!

and when he tired of such antics and of spouting nonsense,
he returned to the tree and told Azarías,

undo the swing and come down, Azarías, it's a loss this
morning, we'll try our luck again this afternoon,

and Azarías collected the gear and climbed down, and as
they crossed the sunny hillside, on their way back to the
Land Rover, a big flock of jackdaws appeared high above
their heads, and Azarías looked up, shaded his forehead
with his hands, smiled, uttered a few inaudible words, and
tapped Señorito Iván on the forearm,

wait a sec,

he said, and Señorito Iván, moodily,

what do you want me to wait for, you useless sack?
and Azarías, drooling, pointed up toward the birds, their screeches softened by the distance,

lots of kiteys, can't you see?
and, without waiting for a reply, he turned his awestruck face toward the sky and shouted through cupped hands,

tchak!!!
and suddenly, to the amazement of Señorito Iván, a jackdaw broke free from the huge flock, and flew straight down toward them in such a beautiful swoop that Señorito Iván grabbed his gun, steadied it on his shoulder, and took aim, and when Azarías saw him, his smile disappeared, his face tightened, panic flashed in his eyes, and he screamed, beside himself,

don't shoot, señorito, it's kitey!
but Señorito Iván felt the hard barrel of the gun caress his cheek, and, desperate after the morning's frustrations, he relished the challenge of shooting a bird plunging straight down like that, and, although he clearly heard Azarías's pleading voice,

señorito, for the love of God, don't shoot!
he couldn't help himself, he had the bird in his sights, he pulled his trigger, and instantly the jackdaw, after a burst of black and blue feathers, tucked its feet in, lowered its head, curled into a ball, and tumbled down, crashing through the sky, and before it hit the ground, Azarías was already sprinting down the hillside, his eyes bulging out of their sockets, careening through the rockroses and bracken, the cage of blind pigeons bouncing noisily against his side, and screaming,

it's kitey, señorito! you killed kitey!
and Señorito Iván strode after him, his gun smoking, a grin
on his face,
      what an idiot,
he mumbled to himself before raising his voice,
      don't worry, Azarías, I'll get you another kitey!
but Azarías, sitting by a rockrose on the edge of the trail,
was holding the dying bird in his big hands, its thick warm
blood streaming between his fingers, feeling, in the depths
of its broken little body, its last faint heartbeats, and, bend-
ing over, he whimpered,
      pretty kitey, pretty kitey,
and Señorito Iván, at his side,
      forgive me, Azarías, I simply couldn't stop myself, I swear,
      the disaster this morning messed with my head, you must
      understand,
but Azarías wasn't listening, he pressed his cupped hands
more tightly around the dying bird, as if trying to preserve
its heat, and gazed at Señorito Iván,
      it's dead! kitey is dead, señorito!
he said, and, in that state, holding the jackdaw, he appeared
a few minutes later on the lawn of the Cortijo, and Shorty
Paco came out on his crutches, and Señorito Iván,
      see if you can't get control of your brother-in-law, Paco, I
      killed his bird, and he's acting like a wailer at a funeral,
he chuckled and immediately tried to justify himself,
      you know me, Paco, you know what it's like waiting the
      whole morning and seeing just one bird, right? well, af-
      ter five hours of nothing, out of the blue, that blasted
      jackdaw came hurtling down, what hunter could keep
      his finger still at such a moment, Paco? explain that to

your brother-in-law and tell him not to act like a fag, for
fuck's sake, I'll get him another bird, there's no shortage
of them on the Cortijo,
and Shorty Paco looked back and forth from Señorito Iván
to Azarías, the former with his thumbs in the armpits of his
hunting jacket, his smile as serene as ever, the latter, bent
over himself, sheltering the dead bird in his clasped hands,
until Señorito Iván jumped back into the Land Rover, started
the engine, and called out through the open window,
don't be like this, Azarías, there are far too many of those
scavengers around anyway, I'll be back for you at four,
let's see if it's better this afternoon,
but big teardrops rolled down Azarías's cheeks,
pretty kitey, pretty kitey,
he repeated as the bird stiffened in his hands, and when he
felt it was no longer a body but a lifeless object, Azarías got
up from his low stool and went over to Tiny's crib, and at that
very moment, the girl let out one of her piercing screams,
and Azarías told Régula, rubbing his nose,
hear that, Régula? Tiny's crying because the señorito
killed kitey,
but that afternoon, when Señorito Iván came to pick him
up, Azarías seemed like a new man, he didn't cry or make
a scene, simply packed the cage with the blind pigeons,
the axe, the swing, and an even thicker rope into the boot
of the Land Rover, calmly, as if nothing had happened, and
Señorito Iván laughed,
that rope isn't for the swing, is it, Azarías?
and Azarías,
it's to climb up to the lookout,
and Señorito Iván,

let's get a move on, see if our luck changes,
and he drove out to the mountain trail, wheels in the deep
furrows, and accelerated, whistling merrily,

Ceferino swears to God there were huge flocks flying
around the boundary of El Pollo's land,
but Azarías seemed to be somewhere else, gazing beyond
the windshield, his thick hands folded over his buttonless
pants, and Señorito Iván whistled an even livelier tune when
he saw him so passive, but the second they arrived, he saw a
flock and went crazy,

for fuck's sake, hurry up, Azarías, can't you see them,
there must be more than three thousand stock pigeons,
the bitches, can't you see how black the sky is over the
holm oaks?
and he rushed to get the guns out, and the cartridge case,
and tied the leather pouches around his waist, and filled the
pockets of his hunting jacket,

look alive, for fuck's sake, Azarías,
he repeated, but Azarías was calmly piling the gear next
to the Land Rover, and he put the cage of blinded pigeons
by the foot of the tree and climbed up the trunk with the
axe, the rope around his waist, and once he was on the first
sturdy branch, he leaned down toward Señorito Iván,

can you hand me the cage, señorito?
and Señorito Iván lifted up the cage of blinded pigeons and,
at the same time, raised his head, and as he did that, Azarías
dropped the rope with the sliding knot around his neck and
pulled the end tight, and Señorito Iván, trying to avoid drop-
ping the cage and hurting the blind pigeons, unaware, tried
to throw off the rope with his left hand,

what the hell are you doing, Azarías, didn't you see that
cloud of pigeons over El Pollo's holm oaks, you idiot fag?

and as soon as Azarías had looped the end of the rope over the señorito's head and then around the branch, he pulled with all his might, groaning and slobbering, and Señorito Iván lost his footing, felt himself suddenly hoisted into the air, dropped the cage, and

for Christ's sake . . . are you crazy?

he said hoarsely, the words so slurred they were barely audible, though the harsh rattle that followed sounded loud and clear, like a protracted snore, and almost immediately Señorito Iván stuck his tongue out, a long, thick, purple tongue, but Azarías wasn't even looking, he simply held the rope, the end of which he now tied to the sturdy branch on which he was sitting, and he rubbed his hands together as he broke into the silliest of smiles, but Señorito Iván, or the legs of Señorito Iván, were still twitching as if he were being electrocuted, as if dancing of their own accord, and his body swayed in empty space for a while until it finally went still, chin on chest, eyes bulging out of their sockets, arms dangling limply down, while up above, Azarías drooled and laughed idiotically at the empty sky, at nothing at all,

pretty kitey, pretty kitey,

he repeated, and at that precise moment, a dense flock of pigeons whooshed through the air, skimming the top of the holm oak where he was hidden.

MIGUEL DELIBES (1920–2010), one of Spain's most popular twentieth-century writers, was known for his empathy for the poor and his unwavering celebration of rural Spain and its traditions. Born in Valladolid, he often spent his summers in his mother's hometown, a rural village in Burgos Province. At age seventeen, he joined the Nationalist forces in the Spanish Civil War, and although he never engaged in battle, his personal trauma and that of his generation heavily influenced his later works. Appalled by the level of government repression, he turned against Franco's dictatorship and worked to restore democracy in Spain. While working on the daily newspaper *El Norte de Castilla,* he published his first novel, *The Cypress Casts a Long Shadow* (*La sombra del ciprés es alargada*), which won the 1947 Nadal Prize and established Delibes as a major writer. He went on to write more than twenty novels, which were translated into more than thirty languages. He won numerous awards throughout his career, most notably the Prince of Asturias Award (1982), the National Prize for Spanish Literature (1991), and the Miguel de Cervantes Prize (1993), for his body of work. Despite his success, he lived his life in relative seclusion. His empathy is reflected in his portrayals of city and especially country life, where he wrote of farmers, shepherds, cheesemakers, blacksmiths, and hunters.

PETER BUSH (b. 1946) is a literary translator from Catalan, French, Spanish, and Portuguese. He has held posts as Professor of Literary Translation at Middlesex University and Professor of Literary Translation and Director of the British Centre for Literary Translation at the University of East Anglia and has been a visiting professor at the University of São Paulo, at Boston University, and at Beijing University. A lifelong advocate of literary translation and the translator of over ninety works, he has served as the chair of the Literary Translation Committee, vice president of the International Translators Federation, board member of the American Literary Translators Association, and convener of the Committee for Literary Translation in Higher Education of the Institute of Translation and Interpreting, and he has been an active participant in numerous other organizations working to promote literary translation. His translations have received many honors and awards, including the Premio Valle-Inclán, the Calouste Gulbenkian Portuguese Translation Prize, and the Premi Ramon Llull for Literary Translation from Catalan. He is also the recipient of the Orden del Mérito Civil, awarded by Spain, for his contribution to the creation of cultural dialogue between the United Kingdom and Spain, and the La Creu de Sant Jordi, the most distinguished award given by the government of Catalonia, for the translation and promotion of Catalan literature.

COLM TÓIBÍN (b. 1955) was born in Enniscorthy. He is the author of twelve novels, including *Long Island, The Master, Brooklyn, The Testament of Mary, Nora Webster, House of Names,* and *The Magician.* His work has been shortlisted for the Booker Prize three times, and it has won the Costa Novel Award and the IMPAC Award. He has also published two collections of stories and many works of nonfiction.